"Exactly Who Or What Are You, Ross St. Clair?"

His eyes became hooded. "I'm a man. Just a man."

Diana didn't believe him for a second. "A man who accosts a complete stranger in the airport and claims she's in some kind of danger?"

He went very still. "Give me ten minutes. That's all I ask. If you don't believe me then, at least I can say I tried. At least my conscience will be clear."

She had to admit she was surprised by his outburst. She was also intensely aware of him, of the long lines of his thighs so near to her own beneath the intimate table for two.

She left an eloquent pause, then glanced down at the elegant gold watch on her wrist. "Ten minutes? You'd better start talking, Mr. St. Clair. You're down to nine and a half."

Dear Reader:

Believe it or not, it's been ten years since Silhouette Desire first made its way from us, the publisher, to you, the readers! And what a wonderful ten years it's been. Silhouette Desire stories are chock-full of delicious sensuality combined with deep emotions. Silhouette Desire is romance at its finest.

To celebrate this decade of delight, I'm proud to present our JUNE GROOMS, six stories about men and marriage. Each of these stories is unique: some are about men who marry—and some are about men whose main goal in life is to *avoid* wedded bliss! But all of these romances concern men who finally meet their match in one special woman.

The authors involved are some of the finest that Silhouette Desire has to offer: Ann Major, Naomi Horton, Raye Morgan, Suzanne Simms, Diana Palmer (with the next installment of her MOST WANTED series!) and Dixie Browning (with a terrific *Man of the Month!*). Some of these stories are serious; some are humorous—all are guaranteed to bring you hours of reading pleasure.

As an extra special treat, these six authors have written letters telling what they like about Silhouette Desire and discussing their feelings about romance . . . and marriage.

These books are our anniversary presents to you, our readers. I know you'll enjoy reading JUNE GROOMS as much as I did. And here's to the *next* ten years!

Sincerely,

Lucia Macro
Senior Editor

SUZANNE SIMMS

NOT *HIS* WEDDING!

SILHOUETTE *Desire*®

Published by Silhouette Books New York

America's Publisher of Contemporary Romance

To friends and editors:
Isabel Swift and Lucia Macro

SILHOUETTE BOOKS
300 East 42nd St., New York, N.Y. 10017

NOT *HIS* WEDDING!

ISBN: 0-373-05718-0

First Silhouette Books printing June 1992

All the characters in this book have no existence outside the
imagination of the author and have no relation whatsoever to
anyone bearing the same name or names. They are not even
distantly inspired by any individual known or unknown to the
author, and all incidents are pure invention.

®: Trademark used under license and registered in the United
States Patent and Trademark Office and in other countries.

Printed in the U.S.A.

Books by Suzanne Simms

Silhouette Desire

Moment in Time #9
Of Passion Born #17
A Wild, Sweet Magic #43
All the Night Long #61
So Sweet a Madness #79
Only this Night #109
Dream Within a Dream #150
Nothing Ventured #258
Moment of Truth #299
Not His Wedding! #718

SUZANNE SIMMS

had her first romance novel published thirteen years ago and is "thrilled" to be back at Silhouette Desire. Suzanne has traveled extensively, including a memorable trip to the Philippines, which, she says, "changed my life." She also writes historical romance as Suzanne Simmons and women's fiction as Suzanne Simmons Guntrum.

The author currently lives with her husband, her son and her cat, Merlin, in Fort Wayne, Indiana. *Not His Wedding!* is her twenty-fourth book.

Dear Readers,

This is the tenth anniversary of Silhouette Desire. I was thrilled to be there in the beginning (*Moment in Time,* Silhouette Desire #9), and I'm happy to be here during this special anniversary celebration with my tenth Desire, *Not* His *Wedding!*

My first love, as a reader and as a writer, has always been the short, sensuous romance. The kind of romance you can't put down, the kind of romance you can read at the beach in the summer, or while curled up in front of the fire on a cold winter's afternoon. The kind that takes you into the special world where a man and a woman fall in love.

One of the reasons I write romance novels is because I believe that for each woman there is, somewhere, that one special man; for each man, one woman who is the other and better half of himself. One man. One woman. Meant for each other and no one else. This is at the heart of what makes category romance and Silhouette Desire both special and successful.

Sometimes the attraction between a man and a woman starts on a primitive, physical level. Someone once said that "passion is a sort of fever in the mind." But when passion is mutual, it can be pure magic!

That's the way it is in *Not* His *Wedding!* when Ross St. Clair and Diana Winsted find themselves on a lush, tropical island in the middle of the Pacific Ocean. That's when their relationship heats up and the fireworks begin! I hope you enjoy their story.

Suzanne Simms

One

Weddings were a damn waste of time.

He knew. He'd attended one too many in his life. Crowds of gawking spectators, thousands of dollars thrown away on frilly dresses and fancy tuxedos, the cloying scent of hothouse flowers, mounds of food and an endless river of drink: it was all a damn waste.

From his experience, half the couples never made it past the honeymoon stage, anyway. One taste of reality and *she* went running home to Mommy and Daddy, and *he* to the nearest singles bar.

Weddings, bah humbug.

Still, this one was different, Ross had to admit. Santo Tomas was a small, humble village, and the couple seemed genuinely devoted to each other. And he was, after all, the guest of honor.

The guest of honor. God knew why, he thought, shaking his head. Anyone could have shown these people how to dig a new well. But he knew it wasn't true. It took somebody with know-how, and he was, apparently, that somebody.

The local padre finished gesticulating over the bride and groom. He had performed the wedding mass in the dialect of the region, of which there were literally hundreds in these islands, and concluded in Spanish: *"¡Dios le bendiga!"*

Everyone from Santo Tomas had crowded into the small church for the ceremony. With the *bendición* they all streamed around the young couple and, along with a flower-decked pagoda containing an image of the village's patron saint, paraded them out into the town square.

It wasn't much of a town square.

The fishing *barrio* was primarily raised houses of split rattan, *sawali,* with thatched roofs, situated along a muddy brown river that had no name. At least this area didn't have the swamp rats that made life on the frontier in Cotabato so hazardous, and the crocodile, once numerous in the chain of seven-thousand-plus islands that made up the Philippines, had some time ago been hunted into local extinction.

At least that's what the *taos* had told him. Ross St. Clair only hoped that the local peasants weren't teasing poor "Joe." The older members of the isolated community still remembered the first Americans to ever set foot on the island: a platoon of GI Joes during World War II. They hadn't seen many Americans since, but the nickname had stuck.

The island version of a wedding reception commenced. Food and drink were carried the short distance to the town square from several houses belonging to the bride's family. Everything was spread out along colorful cloth-covered tables. A few local musicians had brought their instruments; they began to play. The dancing started. Several dogs barked loudly when a group of boys lit a fiery Catherine's wheel, named for the martyred saint, and suddenly it was a cross between a fiesta, a cockfight and the Fourth of July.

"Hey, Joe," shouted one of the men in his limited English, "you want drink?"

The man's name was Cebu and he had no teeth. Seventy-five years old according to some in Santo Tomas, maybe even older according to others, Cebu had been sitting outside the *sari-sari*—the general store—for the past ten years, smoking, drinking fermented coconut juice or the juice of sugarcane and telling his stories to the village children. He was a great favorite with the children.

"Thank you, Cebu. I will gladly drink with you and we will celebrate this day together," answered Ross in the island's native dialect.

The villagers had been surprised and pleased by how quickly he had learned their language. He'd also picked up a smattering of Tagalog, the basis of one of two official languages of the Philippines—the other being English—and several regional dialects, including Cebuano.

Hell, hadn't his professors back in college always said he had a gift for languages?

"Perhaps you will stay in Santo Tomas and take a bride of your own one day?" teased the old man as they sat and drank the local brew.

"I am too young to marry," claimed Ross with a less than solemn face.

One of their fellow revelers called out, "How old are you, Joe?"

"I am thirty-four," he replied.

At that, Cebu cackled and pointed out, gesturing with both hands, "The bridegroom of my wife's greatniece is only twenty. You are not too young."

Ross St. Clair tipped his cup, drank deeply, wiped his mouth with the back of his hand—displaying his appreciation for the homemade liquor—and proceeded to contradict himself. "Then I am too old."

"You are not *viejo*—Cebu is *viejo*," said yet a third man in Filipino English, that distinctive mixture of English, Spanish and localisms.

They all laughed again, more coconut wine was poured and the wedding celebration continued.

Ross St. Clair picked up his cup of coconut alcohol and started toward the beach on the far side of the island.

He had done his duty as the guest of honor. He had proposed the official wedding toast to the bride and groom. He had eaten until he could eat no more. He had danced the native dances. He had listened to the ritual verses or riddles, and he had applauded loudly when the bridegroom sang a favorite ancestral song: the *kundiman*, the greatest of Filipino love songs. Now it was early evening, the light was beginning to fade, and he had a sudden and fierce desire to see the sunset.

Sunset was a brief, brilliant spectacle lasting only minutes on this island, this jut of ancient volcanic mountain that rose from the Celebes Sea and sat so close to the equator. He had better hurry, or he would miss it.

He made his way along a well-trodden path that cut through the thick, green jungle vegetation. Ahead of him, there was an occasional glimpse of pure blue water. He could smell the salt and almost feel the sun-warmed sand beneath his bare feet. He made himself a promise: he would take off his boots as soon as he reached the beach.

The wild native orchids that grew everywhere on the island flapped in his face. There were a dozen varieties and more. He filled his lungs with their exotic dewy fragrance. He walked faster; he was nearly there now.

That's when he saw the yacht.

It was long and sleek, dazzling white and obviously very expensive. And it was anchored offshore.

Ross stopped dead in his tracks.

Strangers were suspect in this part of the world until a man could determine if they were friend or foe. Under the circumstances, the jungle provided him with a natural camouflage that he wasn't eager to part with as yet. His brain seemed to clear instantly. Every one of his five senses went on red alert. He cocked his head and listened.

Voices.

He moved closer and peered between the leaves of a buri palm. There were two men standing together on the beach; they were engaged in an animated conversation. First one spoke, then the other. Arms were occasionally waved. Heads were shaken. They appeared to be negotiating. Several others—guards from the looks of the semiautomatic weapons they carried—were posted farther down the coastline, and a third was patrolling near the area where Ross crouched.

It didn't take a Philadelphia lawyer to figure out these men were not islanders.

He studied the two who were doing all the talking. The one facing him was dressed in pretentious yachting gear, including the pseudo-captain's cap on his head and the designer boat shoes, sans socks, on his feet.

The second man was wearing brown dress slacks and a short-sleeved white shirt. His hair brushed his collar each time he moved his head. His back was to Ross.

He inched closer.

They were speaking English.

"She doesn't know a damn thing about it, I tell you," vowed the one in the brown slacks.

The other man growled in a voice that sounded like he'd smoked a dozen Havana cigars already that day, "Make sure it stays that way."

A nervous gesture, a softly spoken expletive, then he said, "Don't worry, I'll take care of Diana."

The sometime yachtsman grunted once, then again, as if he were still skeptical, and inquired, "When does her flight get into Manila from L.A.?"

"Wednesday."

"Then we expect the 'merchandise' to be in our hands by the end of the week."

"It will be, I promise."

"It'd better be, or Ms. Winsted will pay the price with her lovely head."

Ross froze in place. Pay the price with her lovely head? Was it merely a figure of speech or a genuine threat?

"There's no need to make threats, Carlos," countered the younger of the two men by Ross's calculations. "The delivery will be made on time."

Delivery?

Delivery of what? Drugs? Contraband? Counterfeit money? Diamonds? Ross St. Clair's imagination began to run wild.

He immediately brought himself up short. He was crazy, or well on his way to madness, seeing drug smugglers behind every bush. Maybe he'd been out here too long. Maybe he'd gone native and hadn't even realized it.

No time to worry about that now. He had to get an identification on the two men if he could. Unfortunately they were both silhouetted against the setting sun; it prevented him from getting a good look at them.

Ross quickly scanned their individual heights, body sizes and shapes. The one dressed like a fanciful sailor was short, slightly stocky and had black hair. His eyes were concealed behind tinted sunglasses. Between the dark lenses and the white nautical cap, there wasn't much he could determine about the man's facial characteristics.

His companion was taller, at least six-one, and built like a quarterback. There was little else he could discern about the man.

"C'mon, c'mon, turn around, or at least give me a profile," whispered Ross, knowing full well that he couldn't be heard over the sound of the waves washing ashore.

Damn, he was losing the daylight fast. Worse, the visitors seemed to have concluded their business. They shook hands, and the stocky one walked back to the motorized launch beached fifty yards upshore. His guards followed. They got in the boat, pushed off, started the engine and headed directly for the anchored yacht. There was a name stenciled on the side, but he couldn't make it out from this distance.

What he wouldn't give for a pair of binoculars about now! Ross growled once or twice in exasperation.

The other man made a beeline for a small seaplane waiting for him farther along the coastline. Within five minutes, maybe less, the beach was deserted. It was as though no one had ever been there.

Ross realized then that darkness had descended on the island while he was busy watching the strangers. He'd missed the sunset, after all.

"I wonder what that was about," he speculated, stepping out from behind the palm tree. "And just what in the hell am I supposed to do about it?"

He answered his own question. Nothing. Nada. He wasn't going to do a damn thing. It was none of his business. Diana Winsted was none of his business. The whole undoubtedly sordid, and very probably illegal, business was none of his business. He didn't owe anyone anything. He was keeping his nose clean. He was keeping his nose out of it. That was final.

Was there any real threat to the woman?

Ross shook his head and tried to reason with himself. It didn't matter. He was out of the business of rescuing damsels in distress. Hell, he'd never even been in the business of rescuing damsels in distress. But he was no longer Mr. Nice Guy, who always did the right thing. He was no longer Ross St. Clair, dutiful son of the socially prominent Rachel and Matthew St. Clair of Phoenix and the San Fernando Valley.

He was a grungy jack-of-all-trades with a gift for languages and a knack for fixing things that were broken. He wandered the world, moving from job to job, village to village, country to country. He owed no man or woman his allegiance. He could come and go as he bloody well pleased. He was free, by God. He was free.

Two months ago he'd taken a boat from Manila to this particular island on a whim. He had stayed on a whim, and then to do a job. That job was completed. The village had a new well from which to draw its drinking water. There was no reason for him to remain any longer. He could move on, he should move on, as soon as he decided in which direction he was headed.

But the conversation he'd overheard on the beach would not leave Ross be. He replayed it mentally again and again. The older man's threatening words niggled at him. *Ms. Winsted will pay the price with her lovely head.*

Was she lovely? he wondered.

Then he remembered something the other man had claimed: *She doesn't know a damn thing about it.*

Was she innocent, as well?

Could he just walk away and pretend that he knew nothing of the threat or Ms. Winsted's possible fate? Could he stand by and watch an unsuspecting woman pay with her life? Had he sunk that low? Had he become that uncaring?

Something his parents had drummed into him over the years about people—girls and women, in particular—came to mind: "Let your conscience be your guide, Ross."

Did he still have a conscience? Had he retained any of the socially redeeming qualities that he had been raised with?

Apparently so.

"Damn it all to hell!" muttered Ross St. Clair as he poured out the contents of the cup still clasped in his hand. He watched as the liquid quickly soaked into the white sand at his feet.

It seemed that he knew in which direction he was headed, after all. He was about to make the return trip to Manila. He had a plane to meet.

Two

He was dressed like an unmade bed.

That was Diana Winsted's first impression of the man standing on the other side of airport customs.

He held a makeshift placard against his chest; her name was scrawled across the piece of cardboard in bold, black strokes. She wondered if he'd written it himself. There was something rather emphatic, even uncompromising, about both the man and the hand writing.

She slipped on a pair of designer sunglasses and waited patiently for her passport to be examined and returned. It was also the perfect opportunity to study the stranger without his knowledge.

He didn't look like a chauffeur or one of the company's business associates, so she mentally crossed off the first two possibilities on her list.

What he looked like—Diana was amazed to find herself even giving it a second thought—was a soldier of fortune. Or how she imagined a soldier of fortune would look, anyway.

His brown hair was slightly shaggy and streaked with blond at the temples; it was too long where his shirt collar brushed up against it at the nape. His skin was tanned a deep, unfashionable bronze. Apparently he hadn't heard about the dangers of melanoma, or else a good sunscreen wasn't in common use wherever he'd been spending his time.

There was at least a two-day's growth of beard on his face, but it wasn't enough to disguise a jaw that had been chiseled out of granite. The nose was a tribute to the ancient Romans, with a touch of the aristocratic thrown in for good measure. His eyes had squint lines at the corners; she couldn't make out their color from this distance, but the enigmatic expression in them was unmistakable.

He was wearing wrinkled khaki—damp from perspiration or rain, she couldn't tell which, since it was the wet season in this part of the world—and quasi-military boots, minus the military spit and polish. He had a well-worn canvas knapsack slung over one broad shoulder. Something told her that the man traveled light, very light, indeed, and the knapsack undoubtedly contained all of his worldly possessions.

She, on the other hand, was traveling with four matching pieces of Louis Vuitton. She'd had the sense to leave the rest of her luggage at home.

The customs official stamped her passport and handed it back with a polite smile. "Welcome to the

Philippines, Miss Winsted. We hope you enjoy your visit.''

She gave him an equally polite thank-you in return, and began to collect her bags, signalling for a porter.

The man in wrinkled khaki immediately stepped forward. "Diana Winsted?"

"Yes."

He didn't bother to shake her hand; he just grabbed her by the elbow and steered her away from customs, leaving her luggage and an astonished porter in their wake.

Lowering his voice, he said very clearly, "You— *we*—have to get out of here."

She tried to shake free of his grasp, but his fingers were like a vise around her arm. "I beg your pardon."

He spoke out of the side of his mouth. "I'll explain later."

Diana told herself to remain calm, not to panic. What could possibly happen to her in a huge public airport? *A huge public airport that was halfway around the world from home,* a little voice reminded her.

"You will explain right now, this very instant," she informed him in no uncertain terms. The fact that the man's accent labeled him as a fellow American didn't excuse his behavior. "Are you with Yale's company? Where is Yale, anyway? Why isn't he here to meet me himself?"

"Yale?"

"My fiancé, Yale Grimmer."

"Never heard of him."

Diana dug in her heels and attempted to bring them both to a screeching halt. "Now, wait just a darn minute, Mr.—"

"St. Clair. Ross St. Clair."

He didn't look like a Ross St. Clair to her. He looked like a Mack Bolan. Or a soldier of fortune. Or the spy who came in from the rain. Or a cowboy dressed up in khakis.

Held close to him as she was, Diana found his eyes unavoidable. They were the oddest color. Not blue. Not green. Not brown. But a combination of all three. She had seen the identical coloring once in a piece of polished agate.

There was a keen intelligence in the agate-colored eyes, as well. That surprised her.

Still, her own eyes narrowed, she demanded, "Where are you from?"

"Phoenix."

"Phoenix?"

"Arizona."

"I know where Phoenix is, Mr. St. Clair." After a moment Diana gritted through her teeth. "I suppose that explains it."

"Explains what?"

She sniffed, and with a certain show of indignation, said, "The cowboy attitude."

He laughed, but there was no mirth in his laughter. "Cowboy attitude?" He gave his head a shake. "Where do you come from?"

"Grosse Pointe."

"Grosse Pointe?"

"Michigan."

"I know where Grosse Pointe is, Ms. Winsted."
Then he muttered something under his breath.

"I beg your pardon."

"I suppose that explains it."

"Explains what?" Hadn't they been through all of
this once before?

Ross St. Clair sniffed, perfectly mimicking her own
show of indignation. "The debutante attitude."

She felt the heat rise to her face. "I am not a debutante."

His eyes bored into hers, two chips of hard, variegated stone. "Well, that makes two of us. I'm not a
cowboy."

She could see he was steering her toward the nearest exit. "This has gone quite far enough, Mr. St.
Clair. You're hurting my arm. You will release me
immediately."

To her astonishment, he did.

He hadn't really hurt her, but she did rub her skin,
trying to get her circulation going again. "I am going
back to collect my luggage and locate the driver who
was no doubt sent to the airport by my fiancé."

"Like I said, we have to get out of here."

"Mr. St. Clair—"

"Ross."

"Mr. St. Clair, I have been traveling for twenty-five
hours straight. I have been in four taxi cabs, five air-
ports and at least six time zones since I left home yesterday. Consequently I no longer have a sense of
humor. I seem to have lost it somewhere over the Pacific Ocean." She tapped the toe of her Maud Frizon
pump. "You are either playing a rather bad practical

joke on me, or you're crazy. Frankly I don't care which. I'm tired and I'm hungry and I'm not going one more step anywhere with you."

He stopped, then paced back and forth in front of her for a minute, running his hands through his hair in an agitated gesture and stating unequivocally, "You are in danger."

She raised an eyebrow. "Only from you."

"Not from me, dammit," he swore, seemingly out of frustration. "I'm the one person you can trust."

She pointed out, with what she considered impeccable logic, "You are a total stranger, Mr. St. Clair. You show up here at the airport and tell me I'm in danger. You push me around and you manhandle me. There is no earthly reason why I should trust you."

He lifted his broad khaki shoulders. "Look, lady, I've traveled for three days and three nights by boat, train, plane, bus and jeepney—" he ticked the various modes of transportation off on his fingers as if they were items on a shopping list "—in order to reach the airport in time. I have met every damn flight coming in from Los Angeles since midnight. Consequently *I* no longer have a sense of humor. I realize it sounds crazy, but you are in danger. Whether you believe me or not, you've got trouble, Ms. Winsted. Big trouble."

"In case you hadn't noticed, the only trouble I'm having is with you," she said neatly. "Now you'll have to excuse me, but I intend to find my porter and reclaim my bags."

"Listen—"

"Keep away from me, or I will scream bloody murder." Diana meant every word. Losing her dignity was one thing, but this was turning out to be serious business. This bordered on kidnapping. "I can and I will. Trust me."

He swore under his breath.

Diana turned on her heel and purposefully walked away from him, her spine straight, her posture perfect, her dignity intact. She didn't look back.

To hell with her, Ross decided as Diana Winsted turned on her heel and marched away from him, her silk-clad back ramrod straight.

God knows, he had done his duty. He'd tried to warn her of the possible danger she faced. She just didn't want to hear what he had to say.

Too bad. She had possibly the best pair of legs he'd ever seen on a woman. They were like those of a thoroughbred: long and sleek and lovely to watch in motion.

Still, he'd known Diana Winsted's type before. They tended to be a real pain in the butt.

Ross watched her retreating from across the entire length of the Metro Manila Airport. A frown creased his brow. What had he called her earlier that had gotten her so riled? A debutante? Yup, that was it: a debutante.

She was, too.

Gut instinct told him that Diana Winsted was one of those women who spent their lives perfecting the "niceties" of correct social behavior. The kind considered essential among the "upper" classes, among "old money." She undoubtedly knew which fork to use to eat seafood, what kind of glassware was appropriate to serve an after-dinner liqueur in and whether protocol called for a U.S. senator or a monseigneur to be seated to the hostess's right.

She dressed to absolute perfection, and with nary a wrinkle. He imagined, too, that her hair and makeup were always immaculate, whether the temperature outside was sixty or a hundred in the shade. She had the classic good looks—the cool, chic, haughty blond beauty—of an Alfred Hitchcock heroine.

Another thought suddenly occurred to Ross. This one brought a speculative smile to his face. Perhaps like the Hitchcock movie heroines, there was a passionate and sensuous woman beneath the cool, chic facade....

Either way—icy debutante or warm, sensuous woman—who did he think he was kidding? One half-hearted attempt to warn Diana Winsted of the danger she was in wasn't enough. He had to give it another try.

With that, Ross turned to follow his quarry and, in the process, caught a glimpse of his own reflection in the glass of an airport window.

He hesitated, staring at himself for a moment. Who could blame the woman for having her doubts about him? He scarcely recognized himself. He looked like hell.

What he looked like, Ross St. Clair realized with a genuine sense of surprise, was a bum.

First things first, he reminded himself, and the first order of business was finding out the name of the hotel in which Ms. Winsted was staying. To that end he took off after the porter who had handled her luggage. The twenty-dollar bill folded in his palm would buy him the information he required.

Then he was definitely going to get a haircut. And a shave and a shower. Maybe a clean pair of khakis, as well.

Yup, no doubt about it. Debutante or warm, sensuous woman, Diana Winsted had the best pair of legs he'd ever set eyes on.

Three

Diana didn't recognize him at first.

She was sitting at a linen-covered table in the restaurant of the historic Manila Hotel, studying the dinner menu and minding her own business. When she happened to glance up, there he was, standing in the lobby.

Somehow the man stood out from everyone else milling around the hotel entrance. It wasn't just because he was tall. It wasn't just because he had broad, muscular shoulders and a trim, lean waist. It certainly wasn't because he was handsome, he was too tough and too hard to be considered good-looking in the conventional sense.

Then she recognised him. It was the lunatic from the airport. The one who had tried to kidnap her. The one who'd claimed she was in grave danger. Ross St. Clair.

Apparently he was more resourceful than she'd given him credit for. Somehow, some way, he had discovered where she was staying. No doubt he'd bribed the porter who had helped with her luggage. She wouldn't put it past him.

Diana raised her menu to eye level, she could clearly see him, but he wouldn't—with any luck—see her.

She had to admit that *this* Ross St. Clair was a definite improvement on the "first" one. He'd taken time to get a haircut, although the brown hair, streaked blond by the sun and the sea, was too long by most corporate standards. He was completely clean shaven, and his khakis appeared to have been washed and pressed.

Still, there was something fundamentally uncivilized about him. Which added up to one thing in the end: Ross St. Clair was exactly the *wrong* kind of man.

She knew the type well. Hadn't she watched just last year, helpless to do otherwise, as her best friend's heart was broken by falling in love with the wrong kind of man: a man who was irresponsible, a man unwilling to make a commitment, a man addicted to danger and adventure, a drifter?

That was when Diana had vowed she would only fall in love with the *right* kind of man, a man like Yale Grimmer.

Yale had it all, she thought with genuine satisfaction: good looks, a MBA degree from Harvard, enough money but not too much—too much was considered vulgar—social position, career ambitions that included his recent promotion to corporate vice president of operations for Asia and Pacific, and the unreserved approval of her parents.

What more could any woman ask for?

Indeed, Yale lacked only one thing—the right wife at his side.

She would be that wife, Diana had determined several months ago. It was the reason for her trip to the Philippines, the reason she was joining her fiancé halfway around the world from home. Together they were going to find a house and make all the necessary arrangements for their life overseas. They would return to the States at the end of the summer, for just long enough to have the lavish wedding she'd always dreamed of, followed by a two-week Hawaiian honeymoon.

No one was going to interfere with her plans.

"And that includes you, Mr. Ross St. Clair," murmured Diana as she lowered the restaurant menu.

As if the mere mention of his name had somehow conjured up the man, he appeared at her table.

"Where's the boyfriend?" he inquired matter-of-factly.

She took a deep breath, counted to ten and resisted the urge to wave the diamond engagement ring on her left hand in his face. "Yale is not my boyfriend, he is my fiancé."

"Where's the fiancé?"

She tried to appear unruffled. "I don't know for sure."

Ross's tone was one of cold amusement. "Have you lost him already? Or just temporarily misplaced him?"

Diana knew there was a slight edge to her voice as she said, "Neither one. If you must know, there was a note waiting for me when I checked in. Yale has been called away on business. He'll be back in Manila tomorrow."

There was a flash of white teeth. "How fortunate that I happened along, then, or you would have been forced to spend your first night in a new city and a new country all by yourself."

"There are worse things, Mr. St. Clair," she muttered, each word dripping with sarcasm.

"Ross, please." He pulled out the chair opposite hers, sat down and immediately made himself at home. "You don't mind if I join you for dinner, do you? Have you ordered yet? May I recommend the *Lapu Lapu?* It's a very mild white fish native to the Philippines. You won't have a chance to enjoy it anywhere else in the world. It's quite delicious."

"Mr. St. Clair—"

"It's all right. I'll order for both of us." He turned to the uniformed waiter who magically appeared tableside. "We'll start with the fresh seafood bisque, followed by *Lapu Lapu*." He glanced up at Diana. "Do you care for rice?"

She was too astonished by the man's gall to do anything but shrug her shoulders.

Ross continued ordering. "We'll have some of the *pansit* and the *pinakbet*." He frowned, then added, "Perhaps a little later, coffee and fruit."

"*Pansit?*" she repeated once their waiter had gone.

"*Pansit* is a rice-and-noodle dish seasoned with lime and soy sauce. *Pinakbet* is vegetables—green beans, tomatoes, eggplant and okra—flavored with garlic, onion and ginger—three basic spices in most Filipino kitchens.'' He gave her his full attention. ''Did you know that the Tagalog language has at least one hundred sixty different words relating to rice, and every step of its preparation, every nuance?''

''No, I didn't.''

There was an awkward silence.

''How long are you staying?'' asked her dinner companion as if he were an acquaintance, or perhaps even an old friend.

''Staying?''

''Here at the hotel.''

''I don't know.'' She wasn't sure what arrangements Yale had made for her visit.

''General MacArthur headquartered at the Manila Hotel back during the Second World War, you know. Of course, the rooms have been completely refurbished since then. It's very elegant, very first class, very much *the* place to stay.''

Diana unfolded the linen napkin beside her plate and draped it across her lap. ''My fiancé prefers everything to be first class.''

''Including his women?''

She met his insinuating gaze. ''Especially his women.'' Then she asked, a shade haughtily, ''Tell me, Mr. St. Clair, how long have you been out here?''

''Ross.''

She finally gave in and said, ''Ross.''

Her reward was a charming, masculine smile. ''You mean how long have I been in Manila?''

She was merely trying to make polite conversation. "I mean the Pacific, the Philippines, these islands, this general part of the world."

"A while."

From his appearance, it had been more than a while. Ross St. Clair had the look of a man who'd gone native. She continued to probe. "Years?"

He gave his answer some thought. "Not that long." Picking up his soup spoon, he dug into the seafood bisque set in front of him by their waiter. "These islands will change you, Diana, if you stay."

She tried to appear unperturbed. "There's no doubt about it. I am staying."

He shrugged. "Then you'll find that living in this part of the world peels away the veneer of civilization. It cuts right down to the bone and exposes each of us for exactly who and what we are."

She reached for her glass. "And exactly who or what are you, Ross?"

His eyes became hooded. "I'm a man. Just a man."

Diana didn't believe him for a second. "A man who accosts a complete stranger in the airport and claims she's in some kind of danger?"

He went very still. He searched her eyes. The words came out hard and uncompromising. "Give me ten minutes, Diana. That's all I ask. If you don't believe me after I tell you the whole story, at least I can say I tried. At least my conscience will be clear."

Diana opened her mouth to reply, but no sound came out. She had to admit she was surprised by his outburst. She was also intensely aware of him, of the long line of his thighs so near to her own beneath the intimate table for two.

She left an eloquent pause, then heard herself repeat, "Ten minutes?"

"Ten minutes."

Diana glanced down at the elegant gold watch on her wrist. "You'd better start talking, Ross St. Clair. You're down to nine and a half minutes."

Ross stroked the jawline that usually sported several days' growth of beard and mumbled half under his breath, "Where in the hell do I begin?"

"Why not try beginning at the beginning?" suggested his table companion with a sweet, sarcastic smile, a smile that Ross would dearly loved to have wiped off the beautiful face with the age-old male solution: a kiss.

He was abrupt with her. "Too long. Besides, too much is irrelevant. I'll start where you enter the picture."

"An excellent idea, since you only have nine minutes left," she said.

Somehow Diana Winsted managed to be both polite and impolite at the same time. Ross wondered how long it had taken her to perfect that particular social skill.

Then he concentrated on relating his story, beginning with the evening when he had overheard the conversation between the two men on the beach, and concluding with his arrival at the Metro Manila Airport. Under pressure he managed to convey it all in eight minutes flat.

The woman across the table from him glanced down at the plate of *Lapu Lapu* being set in front of her and, when he was finished talking, said in an amused tone, "That is a very interesting and exciting bedtime story, but it is a bedtime story all the same."

The little fool didn't believe him.

He couldn't believe it.

Ross swore softly, then said in what he knew was a blatantly condescending manner, "In case you hadn't noticed, Ms. Winsted, you're one hell of a long way from home. This is the Pacific, not Grosse Pointe, Say-Yes-To-Michigan. Anything *can* and *does* happen here. Things you couldn't imagine happening back home in a thousand years."

He watched as the tips of her ears turned a bright pink. "I'm well aware of that. I'm not totally naive," she informed him.

He didn't mince words. "Everything I've told you is the absolute truth."

The food was aimlessly pushed around on her plate with a silver fork. "I don't doubt *you* believe it is."

Ross choked on a bite of fish. "You think I imagined the whole incident? That I'm some kind of crackpot?"

The arch of a blond eyebrow said it better than words ever could. The woman shrugged her silk-clad shoulders. "Either that, or yours is the most inventive approach a man has ever taken with me."

His jaw dropped in amazement. "Are you accusing me of trying to pick you up?"

She avoided his direct gaze, rested her chin on one hand and admitted, "The thought had occurred to me."

Ross leaned back in his chair. He blew out his breath expressively. "Good grief." Then he sat up. "How old are you, anyway?"

Diana Winsted was taken aback but nonetheless answered. "Twenty-six."

He shook his head. That explained a lot. She was even younger than he'd thought. It must be the sophisticated hairstyle that had been misleading. If all that long, blond silky stuff was hanging loose around her shoulders, she'd probably look about twenty.

The question popped out of his mouth. "You sleeping with Grimmer?"

"I beg your pardon."

He repeated, slightly louder, "Are you sleeping with Yale Grimmer?"

"Shh—I'm not hard of hearing. Now everyone is staring at us," she whispered.

He didn't bother to turn his head to see if anyone was really looking. "Makes no difference to me."

"It does to me," she shot back, obviously embarrassed by his outburst.

"Well, are you?"

Her golden-brown eyes flashed with anger. She lowered her voice and carefully enunciated each and every word. "It is none of your damn business."

She wasn't.

She was, however, hot under the collar.

Diana Winsted continued, "The next thing I know you'll be inquiring after my underwear size."

He zeroed in on her full, rounded breasts. "Thirty-four C." He dropped his gaze lower. "Panties, a five." His eyes swept up the length of her lovely body. "Dress, size eight, maybe a ten, since you're fairly tall. I'd estimate five feet six inches, one hundred twenty-five pounds."

The expression on her face told him that he was close. Real close.

The aristocratic nose was raised a notch higher. "I won't ask how you know."

Ross enthusiastically dug into his *Lapu Lapu*. It was a minute, maybe two, before he volunteered, "Engineer."

"Engineer?"

"I was trained as an engineer."

Her features were a study in skepticism. They said loud and clear, *Right. And if you expect me to believe that one, I know of a nice island for sale cheap.*

"The fish is delicious, you were right about one thing," his dinner companion commented, taking delicate bites of her *Lapu Lapu* and vegetables.

Meaning he was wrong about everything else.

Meaning he was wasting his time.

"Somehow, some way, I'm going to resist saying 'I told you so.' But mark my words, you will be sorry one day," Ross informed her as he finished his meal.

She came back with, "I'm already sorry."

"About what?"

"If you must know, I'm sorry I ever listened to you. I'm sorry I ever allowed you to sit down and have dinner with me." She put the linen napkin down on the table and rose to her feet. "You'll have to excuse me, Mr. St. Clair, assuming that is your name, of course. I have some unpacking to do and I intend to go to bed early tonight.''

''Don't let me stop you,'' drawled Ross, taking a leisurely sip of his coffee.

''I won't.'' She took one step toward the entrance-way of the restaurant, then threw over her shoulder, ''Good night and goodbye.''

''Adios to you, too, lady,'' Ross muttered as he downed the last of his coffee.

He stood, dug a few bills out of the pocket of his khakis and tossed them on the table. It seemed he was buying dinner tonight. Then he exited the restaurant, taking his own good time.

What a waste.

All that beauty, all that charm, all that woman wasted on a man like Yale Grimmer. Not that it was any of his business. It wasn't. Hell, they probably deserved each other. Yale and Diana, a match made in heaven.

He was standing beneath the towering front portico of the Manila Hotel, trying to decide if he should take a cab or walk back to his own lodgings, when he distinctly heard someone call out his name.

''Mr. St. Clair. Ross St. Clair.''

He nonchalantly looked around and saw Diana Winsted hurrying toward him, her high heels clicking on the polished floor of the lobby.

He tried very hard not to gloat. ''Yes?'' he said when she got closer.

Her breath was coming in little gasps; apparently she'd been running, or the next thing to it. "Mr. St. Clair—"

"Ross."

"Ross." She tried to catch her breath. "Maybe your story isn't as crazy as I first thought."

A masculine brow was arched into an inverted V. "Come to your senses already, have you?"

"You might say so." The young woman nervously wetted her lips with the tip of her tongue and wrung her hands in front of her. "It's my room."

"Your room?" The tiny hairs on the back of Ross's neck stood straight on end. Every one of his five senses went on red alert, just as they had that evening on the beach. "What about your room?"

"Someone has ransacked it."

Four

"Holy—" Ross caught himself just in the nick of time "—smokes!"

The beautiful, sophisticated blonde beside him sighed and agreed in a voice that trembled with emotion, "It's not a pretty picture, is it?"

They paused in the connecting doorway between the sitting room and the bedroom of the luxurious hotel suite. Chairs were haphazardly overturned. Suitcases were flung open. Drawers and closet doors stood ajar. Clothes were strewn everywhere.

It was, in short, an ungodly mess.

Ross let out a low whistle. "It looks like a professional job to me."

"A professional job?" echoed Diana.

He ventured into the bedroom, carefully stepping over a slip in taupe silk puddled at his feet. "Got to hand it to them, they were thorough." For some reason he thought of the goons on the beach, the ones with the fancy weapons. "What do you think?"

Diana looked at him and threw up her perfectly manicured hands. "What do *I* think? *I* think someone has just turned my hotel room upside down. That's what *I* think."

Ross turned and pinned her to the wall with his rock-hard gaze. "Why?"

With an air of innocence that he doubted even a consummate actress could fake, she swallowed and admitted, "I don't know."

His gaze settled on a pink nightgown tossed unceremoniously on the floor alongside the bed. Something, some sixth sense, some gut-level instinct, told him that Diana Winsted never tossed anything unceremoniously on the floor. He imagined that everything had its place and everything was in its place before the goon squad had arrived and rearranged her belongings. "Is anything missing?"

She shrugged.

"Do you want me to call hotel security?"

Her expression grew bleak. "I don't know."

"The police?"

She said, even bleaker, "I don't know."

"What do you want to do?"

In unison, they said, "I don't know."

"I suggest we skip the official red tape—it can get pretty sticky at times—and try to determine if anything has been taken ourselves." Ross bent over and snared a lacy bra from the arm of a chair. It dangled from his index finger by one flimsy strap. "I think we can safely assume that whoever trashed the room wasn't after your underwear.''

Diana snatched the bra from his grasp. ''You seem to spend an inordinate amount of time speculating about my lingerie, Mr. St. Clair.''

He expelled a breath of self-deprecating laughter and said softly, ''Yeah, well, maybe it's been a while since I've seen pretty things like yours.''

Her eyebrows rose fractionally. She seemed to be biting her tongue. Literally. Then she quickly went about the business of tidying the room.

Ross put the furniture back to rights, then sat down in an elegantly upholstered chair, crossed one leg over the other and rested his hand on his boot. There wasn't anything to do but watch Diana, so that's exactly what he did. Every movement the woman made was smooth and fluid, poetry in motion. Whatever else might be true about her, Ms. Winsted was a pleasure to watch, he acknowledged.

She also made him feel like a bull in a china shop.

''Nothing has been torn or damaged,'' she reported as the last dress was hung in the closet.

''What about your jewelry?''

''I only brought a few pieces with me on this trip, but it all seems to be here,'' she informed him as she went through the pile of necklaces and earrings that had been dumped in the middle of the bed.

''Money?''

''Most of it was in my handbag, although I always keep extra in my suitcase. It's here, as well.''

''Traveler's checks?''

''The same.''

She double-checked a leather travel kit that was decidedly masculine in appearance, sorting through the contents and coming up with an engraved silver brush set, diamond-studded cuff links and matching tie tack, a book or two, a carefully wrapped bottle of expensive Scotch and a pipe.

"Thank God, they didn't steal your pipe," Ross offered in a droll tone.

Diana stood a little straighter and looked down her nose at him. "It isn't my pipe." She went on, "Yale asked me to bring a few of his things that he'd forgotten."

Ross leaned back into the cushions and slowly stroked his jaw. "I don't get it."

"It's very simple. He was packing in a hurry and he overlooked a few items," she explained.

"No, no, I don't mean your boyfriend's stuff." Ross wiped away any consideration of Yale Grimmer with a wave of his hand. "I don't get what it was the thieves were after. If this was your average, run-of-the-mill breaking and entering, why didn't they take your money and jewelry?" Damn, he was stumped, and he didn't like being stumped. "It doesn't make any sense."

Diana sank down on the edge of the mattress and began to methodically refold her lingerie, the gold charm bracelet on her wrist clinking with each movement of her hand. "It doesn't make any sense, does it?" She brightened. "Unless it was vandalism."

Ross shook his head.

"The thieves broke into the wrong room and didn't realize their mistake until it was too late?"

Ross shook his head again.

"They broke into my room and discovered there wasn't anything worth stealing?"

"I don't think so, Diana. The men I overheard on the beach mentioned you by name in conjunction with what they called the 'merchandise.'"

"The 'merchandise'...?" Her voice trailed off.

"Could anyone have slipped a package into your bags without your knowledge?"

Her eyes grew huge and apprehensive; her voice became a mere whisper. "Are you suggesting that someone may have tried to use me as a courier?"

That's exactly what he was suggesting, but he said, "Maybe."

She slowly shook her head from side to side. "I don't see how. My luggage was locked at home and checked onto my flight as soon as I reached the airport. I have the only set of keys."

Ross weighed her answer, then inquired, "Do you happen to know a man named Carlos?"

"Carlos? I don't think so. No." Diana rubbed her temples. "You're giving me a headache, Mr. St. Clair."

"And here I thought I was only a pain in the—"

The shrill ring of the telephone on the bedside table interrupted him.

They both jumped.

"You'd better answer that."

Diana picked up the receiver and managed a calm enough "Hello?" A frown of concentration settled on her face. "I'm having trouble hearing you. We don't have a very good connection. Is that you, Yale?" She paused and listened. "I see. Yes, I understand. Where are you now? Port Man-what? Port Manya. Of course I will. Just let me get something to write on." A pointed look was directed at Ross.

"You want me to leave?" he mouthed.

The blonde shook her head and made a gesture with her hand.

"You want paper and pen?"

She nodded. He rummaged around in the drawer on his side and found what was needed.

Then Diana spoke into the telephone again. "You'll have to repeat that information, Yale." She jotted down several words and numbers. "I've got it. Asian Air. Tomorrow morning at nine-thirty. The flight to Port Manya. My ticket will be waiting for me at the airport."

Ross blatantly eavesdropped. It was impossible not to overhear Diana's side of the conversation.

She was visibly straining to hear the man on the other end. "Yes, I'm wearing it. I never take it off. You know that."

They must be talking about the engagement ring he'd noticed on her left hand.

"All right. I'll meet you tomorrow evening at the hotel on Port Manya." Her back was turned to Ross. "Yes, I . . . Yale? Yale?" She held the receiver a good foot away from her, stared at it for a minute and finally hung up, announcing, "We were cut off."

Ross tapped his index finger against his bottom lip. "It's the telephone system. Sometimes it works." He shrugged. "Sometimes it doesn't. Never can tell in this part of the world. Like the electricity. It's a crap shoot."

"Thank you for reassuring me," Diana said with a small stoic laugh.

"I take it the boyfriend isn't returning to Manila tomorrow, after all."

"As you no doubt heard, my fiancé has made arrangements for me to join him on the island of Port Manya."

Ross flicked at a clump of dried dirt clinging to the heel of his boot and watched as it landed on the pale blue carpeting. "Business before pleasure?"

She wasted no time in informing him, "Yale has a great deal of responsibility as a corporate vice president. He can't simply drop his work to come after me."

"Which translates into 'business before everything but business,'" he said curtly.

Her lips tightened. "I doubt if you would understand."

"Don't be too sure of that," muttered Ross. He unfolded his long legs, stretched out his feet and nudged the clump of dirt with the toe of one boot. "The man's a fool."

Diana responded in a vexed way, "I beg your pardon."

He didn't care what it sounded like to her; it was time she heard the truth. "Your fiancé is a damn fool to let a woman like you run around on your own. It only spells one thing—trouble. Big trouble."

Her eyes were squinted in anger. "What it spells, Mr. St. Clair, is m-a-l-e c-h-a-u-v-i-n-i-s-t."

He'd been called worse. A lot worse.

He pushed the dried dirt under the bed. Then he gave her a long, measuring look. "You didn't mention to Yale that your room had been ransacked."

"I saw no reason to worry him. There's nothing he could do, anyway." One by one she fingered the charms on her bracelet, then she looked straight at him. "Besides, I'm a big girl. I can take care of myself."

"Right." Ross managed not to laugh in her lovely face. "I noticed you didn't tell him about me."

She shot back, in that cultured, sophisticated tone that drove him crazy, "There's nothing to tell."

Ross had the most incredible urge to change all that, to take this beautiful and exasperating woman in his arms and kiss her until she couldn't see straight.

Hell, until *he* couldn't see straight.

Maybe then he'd know. Was she cold only on the outside and all hot and sweet on the inside? Was she an ice princess or a woman of passion? What would she taste like? What would she feel like? What would it be like to make love to her?

Suddenly he had a vision of Diana Winsted, naked, with her long shapely legs wrapped around his body, her breasts pressed to his chest, her blond hair hanging around her bare shoulders, all silky and cool against his hot flesh, her lips slightly swollen from his kisses.

He would leave no stone unturned. There would be no part of her that he would not know intimately. He would bury his mouth in her hair, inhaling her fragrance, even as he buried himself deep inside her.

Feeling the very real and slightly uncomfortable stirrings of sexual arousal, Ross groaned aloud.

This wasn't the right time, or the right place. And it sure as hell wasn't the right woman. He'd obviously been out here too long. He'd been away from women too long. Maybe it was time for him to head back to civilization.

The soft touch of a hand on Ross's arm brought him around. "Are you all right?"

He blinked several times in quick succession and growled, despite plenty of evidence to the contrary, "I'm fine."

"I believe I'm finished in here," said Diana, indicating that the bedroom of her hotel suite had been restored to its former pristine condition.

He tried to take his mind off the vision of her nude body wrapped around him like a tight-fitting glove. "Have you ever flown on Asian Air before?" he inquired as they walked to the door.

"No, I haven't."

"Puddle jumpers."

Her forehead crinkled. "Puddle jumpers?"

"They're small planes that hop from island to island around the Pacific. It's not what you're used to."

She immediately countered with, "You don't know what I'm used to and what I'm not."

Yes, he did. Diana Winsted was obviously a woman who traveled first class all the way. Asian Air should come as something of a surprise to her.

Ah, well, she would learn soon enough for herself.

She extended her hand and said politely, "I want you to know I appreciate your returning to the room with me tonight. And I will take heed of your warning about the two men on the beach."

He took her hand in his, but made no pretense of shaking it. "Watch your back, Diana."

"I will."

"Promise?"

"I promise," she said, smiling at him.

It was the first time he had seen her genuinely smile, and it changed everything. Maybe that was why he did it. Maybe not. He never knew for sure.

Instead of releasing her hand, Ross raised it to his mouth. He fully intended to place an old-fashioned Continental-style kiss on the back. At the last moment he changed his mind. He turned her hand over and brushed his lips lightly across her palm.

He literally felt the quiver that rippled through her, saw the shiver that shook her from her shoulders all the way down to her knees. The tawny eyes darkened. He even caught a glimpse of something deep down inside them. Fire. Golden fire. Maybe even desire. Licking at him like flames of hot honey. But when he took a step toward her, Diana quickly retreated.

He could take a hint. The sign read Hands Off.

He backed out of her hotel suite. "Lock the door after me, and don't forget to hook the chain."

She appeared to be holding her breath. "Yes, Ross."

Dammit, he didn't want to leave. It was the craziest thing. "Are you sure you aren't afraid to stay here alone?"

"I'm sure."

"You know, the thieves must have had a passkey."

"I know. But they won't be back. I don't have whatever they think they want."

He grudgingly agreed. "You're right."

"Yes, I am. This time."

He'd run out of excuses not to leave. He gave her a jaunty little half salute. "Adios, then, Diana Winsted."

She paused with her hand on the doorknob. "Goodbye, Ross St. Clair."

The door closed. Still, he didn't walk away until he heard the lock click into place.

Ross took the long way back to his hotel. Then he undressed and stood under a steaming shower, letting the water run down his traitorous body.

He called himself every name in the book.

Fool.

Nitwit.

Dumb jerk.

Chump.

Diana Winsted wasn't his type. And he certainly wasn't *her* type. Hell, he had purposely left the life he'd known to get away from women like Diana.

That wasn't entirely true.

He had left the life he'd known to get away from the man he had become, to find out if he could survive without the benefit of the St. Clair family name and fortune behind him. That was the truth.

Six months, thought Ross as he vigorously scrubbed every inch of skin from his hair to the soles of his feet. He had spent six bloody months out here in what he called the "real world." Sometimes it seemed like forever. A lifetime or two, at the least. He was tougher. Leaner. Not as polite, but not as mean. He looked inside people, or at least he tried to.

But no one had to look very far beneath the chic, haughty exterior to see that Diana Winsted had all the depth of a wading pool. The woman was definitely *not* his type.

So why couldn't he get her off his mind?

Five

Damn the man!

She'd overslept this morning and it was all Ross St. Clair's fault, Diana grumbled as she hurried through the huge Metro Manila Airport.

It had proved impossible for her to get to sleep after he'd left her hotel room last night. Not because she was afraid the thieves might return. In truth, she wasn't. But because Ross had kissed her hand and for a moment, for one insane moment, she had seen the sexual hunger in his eyes and knew it was merely a reflection of her own wanton desires.

Dear God, even now when she closed her eyes and relived the touch of his mouth, his lips, his tongue, on the sensitive flesh of her palm, she began to feel strange inside. Not at all like herself.

It had been a brief but surprisingly intimate caress. She didn't think a man had ever kissed her in quite that way before. It had left her skin sensitized, her entire body atingle, every nerve ending aware that she was alive, that she was a woman and he was a man. It had never happened to her like that before.

Not even with Yale.

It must never be allowed to happen again. She would not get involved with a man like Ross St. Clair. She was engaged to be married and had been for the past six months. The fact that her fiancé had been overseas for all but one of those months was beside the point.

Her plans were made. The church and the country club had been reserved since last winter. Her designer gown was bought and hanging in her closet at home. The wedding invitations were printed, addressed and ready to be mailed. There was no going back now. Her life was in order, and it would stay that way.

Besides, she and Ross had said good-night *and* goodbye at the door of her hotel room the previous evening.

She had no idea where he was staying in the huge, sprawling city of Manila. She didn't have the foggiest notion of what his plans were. She had no inkling of where the man was coming from or where he was going to.

It's better this way, a small voice inside her head whispered to Diana.

It was better this way. Ross was exactly the *wrong* kind of man for her.

But something told Diana it had been a narrow escape.

The man behind the counter of Asian Air was of indeterminate age and origin. He was gray haired and gray skinned; even his uniform was gray. There was a cigarette dangling from his bottom lip, and one eye was cast in a permanent squint as the gray smoke coiled up into his face.

"You're late, Miss Winsted," he announced as she hurried up to the counter.

"I know. I'm sorry. I had some difficulty in locating you." She wasn't about to confess that she had overslept. And, once she'd reached the airport, it had taken a good forty-five minutes to find Asian Air's single gate.

"Everybody else is on board." She was handed what appeared to be a ticket stub.

"Then I'll check my bags and we can be on our way," she said, turning to the porter behind her. She'd had to plead and cajole and finally bribe him with the promise of a generous tip to get him this far.

The Asian Air agent lit a second cigarette from the stub of the first one still clutched between his yellowing teeth. "'Fraid not."

She turned back. "I beg your pardon."

"You don't check your bags, missy. You carry them onto the plane yourself."

No one had ever called her "missy." Diana didn't like it, not one bit. And she did not carry her own luggage anywhere!

"My good man—" although she seriously doubted it from the looks of him "—I have four matching pieces of Louis Vuitton. I will require both your assistance and the porter's to get them aboard the aircraft." She instilled a certain firmness, a certain authority, into her voice and took control of the situation. "I can manage the carryon. It will be necessary for the two of you to bring the rest."

With that, she picked up the smallest bag and headed for the gate, all the while telling herself that if she didn't look back, that if she didn't show the slightest sign of hesitation, they would follow her like sheep.

Men always did if they were handled correctly.

Confident that the entourage was behind her, Diana briskly walked out onto the tarmac and toward the twin-engine airplane with Asian Air stenciled on the side.

What had Ross called them last night? Puddle jumpers? He was, apparently, right.

Miraculously she managed to get up the rickety steps without breaking her high heels or her neck and, ducking her head, entered the tiny plane.

The first person she saw was Ross St. Clair.

Her mouth dropped open. She quickly snapped it shut again and scanned the aircraft for an empty seat. There was only one, of course. It was right beside Ross's.

She vowed she wasn't going to ask. But in the end, Diana couldn't help herself. Grudgingly she sat down beside him and breathed through clenched teeth. "Tell me, is this one of those incredible coincidences?"

Ross pushed the wrinkled khaki hat back off his face and said, "Nope."

"Then you admit that you're following me?"

"Absolutely," he stated with a deadpan expression.

The gall. The nerve. The absolute cheek of the man. For a moment—just for one tiny forbidden moment—she mentally saw an image of Ross St. Clair's bare backside.

Diana gave herself a good shake. "Why?"

He seemed to throw out the first idea that occurred to him. "Guardian angel?"

A soft hoot. "Not even close."

He tried again. "Bodyguard?"

She rolled her eyes. "Thanks, anyway, but I don't need a bodyguard. I can take care of myself."

"Concerned friend, then?"

"We hardly know one another," Diana felt compelled to point out to him.

The deep masculine voice was bitingly sarcastic. "Concerned stranger?"

She sighed. "You are that."

He appeared casually intrigued. "What?"

"You concern me and you are a stranger."

Apparently Ross wasn't offended. In fact, if anything he seemed amused. He put his head back and laughed heartily. It was a nice laugh, Diana acknowledged.

He made one final attempt to explain his presence. "Let's just say that I'm a concerned fellow American."

"I suppose I can accept that," she remarked after due consideration.

"Once I see you safely into the arms of your boyfriend, I'll grab the next flight out of town."

"Promise?"

"I promise." Ross held up three fingers. "Scout's honor."

She was still skeptical. She looked at him askance. "Were you ever a Boy Scout?"

Ross removed the shapeless khaki hat, crossed his legs and hung it over his knee. "Yup." Then he added, "You'd be surprised by what I've been."

"Shocked is no doubt more like it."

He gazed out the window, then turned back to her and reached for her hand. He held it in his and vowed, "You won't be sorry I'm along."

"I am already," she said, undoing her hand from his.

"Give it up, Diana." He certainly seemed to be in a chipper mood this morning. "For good or for ill, the fates have thrown us together. We'll just have to make the best of it."

They both glanced up as the porter and the Asian Air agent struggled onto the airplane with her luggage.

The agate-colored eyes flickered with mild humor. "I see you're traveling light, as always."

Diana sniffed. "I haven't any idea how long I'll be on Port Manya. I like to be prepared."

"That's my motto—'Be prepared.'"

She just bet it was.

Suddenly Diana craved a cup of coffee. Very black and very hot. And perhaps a croissant, warmed in the oven and spread with a thick layer of apricot preserves. Her mouth started to water. "Does this airplane have a flight attendant?"

"Nope."

Her stomach growled softly, protesting the fact that she'd skipped breakfast. "Will we be served anything to eat or drink?"

Ross slouched down in his seat and made himself comfortable. "Highly doubtful."

She should have guessed. "When do we land on Port Manya?"

He put it into layman's terms. "We get there when we get there."

She made a concerned, involuntary movement of her hands. "But isn't this a regularly scheduled flight?"

Ross turned, his eyes leveled at her. "This part of the world operates by its own set of rules. And rule number one is you get there when you get there and not before."

Diana swallowed the implied insult. "Once he's finished stowing my luggage, I'll ask the ticket agent what time we're scheduled to arrive."

"Ticket agent?"

"The one at the counter. The one helping with my bags," she said loftily.

His mouth twisted into a wry smile. "That's not a ticket agent. That's our pilot."

* * *

Once they were in the air and flying high over a blue ocean dotted with green islands of every size and shape, Ross made an offer she couldn't refuse. He took a thermos from his knapsack, and said, "Would you like to share a cup of coffee?"

"Coffee? Real coffee?"

"Real coffee. I had one of the restaurants in the airport fill my thermos before boarding."

Diana confessed, "I think I'd kill for a cup of coffee right about now."

"I'm glad you warned me," he said, pouring a generous amount of steaming liquid into the thermos lid-turned-cup. "In that case, you go first."

"Oh, but I couldn't," she protested weakly. "I shouldn't. I can't—"

"Sure, you can," Ross assured her as he urged the coffee into her hand.

"Thank you." She took a sip, sat back and sighed contentedly. "I didn't have time for a cup this morning. I overslept."

The instant it was out of her mouth Diana realized she'd made a mistake in telling him.

The agate-colored eyes narrowed. "You had trouble sleeping last night, didn't you?"

She shrugged and tried to pass it off as, "Probably jet lag."

He wasn't convinced. "Maybe."

"Anyway, thanks for the coffee."

He let it go. "You're welcome."

Diana followed his gaze to the diamond engagement ring on the third finger of her left hand.

Ross grunted. "Nice rock."

"Thank you."

"Is it real?"

"Of course it's real." The man really was uncouth!

The mocking look was back in his eyes. "Where we're going, sweetheart, you don't want to flash a diamond like that. Wouldn't be safe. A thief might come along and chop off your pretty little finger to get the stone. You'd better put it away."

Diana suddenly felt half-sick to her stomach, but she still managed to glare at him. "I'm not a child, Ross. I do the same thing when I'm in most cities back in the States, as a matter of fact."

She defiantly turned the ring around on her finger until the diamond was concealed underneath. The stone dug into the tender flesh of her palm, but she refused to give Ross the satisfaction of knowing that.

"Now it looks like a wedding band," he commented, a frown bracketing his mouth.

"It does, doesn't it?" she agreed, studying the thin gold band on her hand.

"You and the boyfriend set a date yet?"

"Yes, we have."

He casually inquired, "When is the big day?"

"The second Saturday in September."

That brought a raised eyebrow. "Here I figured you for a traditional June bride."

"We considered June. Then Yale was promoted to vice president, and the demands on his time increased. We decided September would work into his schedule better."

"Another example of business before everything but business," ventured the man beside her.

"As I said before, I don't think you would understand."

Diana didn't wish to be rude, but what would a drifter like Ross know of responsibility? Of the corporate decisions that Yale had to make each day, decisions that affected hundreds, sometimes thousands of employees?

Her seatmate gave her a quick, penetrating look. "It's going to be a long day. I suggest we try to get some sleep." He plunked the wrinkled khaki hat down on his head, pulling it partially over his face. Within a minute or two, he seemed to be dozing.

Diana put her head back and closed her eyes. She was tired and Ross was right: it was going to be a long day.

Diana awakened gradually.

First she was aware of the loud hum of the aircraft's engines, then the wafting of cool air on her face from a vent overhead and finally, as her eyes blinked open, the fact that the plane was cloaked in deepening shadows.

It was late afternoon.

She turned her head and found Ross St. Clair watching her. "How long have I been asleep?"

"A few hours."

She sat up straight, reached behind her to massage the crick in her neck and gazed out the window. Blue skies, blue sea, dots of green islands. Nothing had changed except the time of day. "Where are we?"

Ross shrugged his broad shoulders. "I don't know exactly. Somewhere over the Pacific. I would guess an hour out from Port Manya."

Diana suddenly realized they were alone. "Where are all the other passengers?"

"They got off at the last stop."

"The last stop?"

He patiently explained. "The plane had to refuel. You slept through the landing and the takeoff."

"And lunch?" she inquired, realizing that the hollow feeling in the pit of her stomach was back.

He nudged his knapsack. "I saved you some."

She shook her head, incredulous. "I can't believe I slept through the whole thing. I must have been exhausted."

"Jet lag. It'll catch up to you like that sometimes."

"Do you think we'll reach Port Manya before dark?"

Ross gave a noncommittal grunt. "Chances are the runway on the island isn't equipped with lights."

"Meaning we have to land while there's still enough daylight for the pilot to see what he's doing."

He rubbed his jaw and frowned in thought. "That's it in a nutshell."

Diana permitted herself a small sigh. "Have you been to Port Manya before?"

"No, but I've been on a dozen other islands just like it. It's a big ocean, the Pacific."

"Yes, it is." She fell silent, then reached out and touched his arm and said in a husky voice, "Thank you, Ross."

He seemed surprised. "For what?"

"For keeping an eye on me while I slept."

"It was nothing."

But he was wrong. It wasn't nothing; it was very definitely something. Where would she be now if he hadn't decided to come along on this trip?

The answer was clear, she would be the lone passenger on a tiny airplane on its way to a godforsaken island in the middle of nowhere.

Diana turned her head and encountered two agate-green eyes staring at her. Ross might be a little rough around the edges, but he was a gentleman all the same.

Before she considered whether it was a good idea or not, she leaned toward him, pressed her lips to his cheek and repeated in a whisper, "Thank you for being a concerned fellow American."

She went to draw back and discovered Ross's hand on her nape, effectively holding her head in place. He didn't force the issue; he just waited to see what she would do next.

It was curiosity, of course, that got Diana in the end. She thought of her trembling reaction to his caress the night before, and all he had done was brush his lips across her palm.

What would it be like to really kiss this man?

That was the question that raced through her veins.

It would only take a minute to find out the answer. All she had to do was lean toward Ross again, and she would run straight into his mouth.

She made an almost imperceptible movement in his direction, and their lips met.

Diana had always thought that kissing was a pleasant enough diversion, although she'd never cared for it in its more intimate forms. She had been called an "ice princess" all the way through high school and college, as much on the basis of her cool blond looks as anything. Despite what everyone thought, she did not have a chunk of cold stone where her heart was supposed to be. It just took her a little longer to warm up to people.

It had all been a lie.

Ross St. Clair brought his mouth down on hers, and Diana burst into flames. Suddenly she was on fire. She was burning white-hot from the inside out, yet her skin was cool to the touch.

It wasn't supposed to be like this, she thought, trying not to panic, trying to retain what little rational mind she had left. She'd kissed the man on a whim, and it had backfired on her. She was in trouble. Big trouble.

"Ross—"

"So your curiosity got the better of you, too?" he murmured as he continued nibbling on her mouth.

"Too?" she echoed.

"I couldn't get to sleep last night," he admitted. "I kept wondering what it would be like to kiss you."

"This is crazy," she said breathlessly.

"Yeah, I know."

"We shouldn't be doing this."

"Probably not."

"We're all wrong for each other."

"I couldn't agree with you more."

"We've got to stop."

"We will."

But they didn't.

Her fingers encircled his neck. His hands found their way around her waist. She parted her lips slightly, and he plunged into her mouth, sipping her, tasting her, devouring her, nipping at her with his teeth, using his tongue to seduce her until she wanted to weep from both joy and sorrow.

God forgive her, it felt so right and yet he was the wrong man. And this was the wrong time and the wrong place.

She finally managed a strangled, "Please, Ross—"

"Please, Ross, what?" he breathed against her feverish skin.

"Please stop."

He paused and stared down at her.

"I—I'm sorry," she stammered. "I shouldn't have kissed you. It was my mistake."

She watched the fire extinguish in his eyes. Within seconds they were once again two hard chips of variegated stone.

The skin on his face seemed to tighten. "My mistake, as well."

She was shaken. "I'm so sorry, Ross."

"So am I, Diana. So am I."

Her eyes traveled reluctantly to his. "I don't know what to say."

"There's nothing to say. We got a little carried away—we went a little crazy. It happens."

"Not to me," she said, bewildered. "It doesn't happen to me."

And suddenly, with a cold pang, Diana thought, *What if it never happens to me again?*

"Sure it happens to you," Ross stated, contradicting her. "You're only human—flesh and blood like the rest of us."

If he only knew. If he only knew. But he must never know. Her hand floated to her breast. "I guess I'm still suffering from jet lag."

He nodded his head. "Right. Jet lag." He turned and gazed out the window of the aircraft. "I think we're coming in on Port Manya now."

Diana quickly straightened her hair, tucking a stray wisp behind her ear, and attempted to put herself to rights, firmly ignoring the fact that her hands were shaking.

She glanced out the window across the aisle from their seats. Her heart gave a leap. "Ross, it's nothing but jungle."

He responded evenly, "Yup, sweetheart, it's a jungle out there."

Six
_____

She took it back. Ross St. Clair was no gentleman.

"Excuse me," Diana called after him as he disembarked and began to walk away from the aircraft.

He paused, glanced back at her over a broad, muscular shoulder—the one without his canvas knapsack casually tossed over it—and said from behind dark aviator glasses, "Yes?"

She stood waiting beside her luggage. It had been dumped on the grass at the side of the runway by their Asian Air pilot. "I need your help."

Ross removed his sunglasses and slipped them into the breast pocket of his khaki shirt. "You do?"

Diana gritted her teeth. The man was deliberately being obtuse. "Yes, I do."

"With what?"

So, he was determined to make it as difficult for her as he could. She should have known he'd insist upon having his pound of flesh.

Diana shifted her weight from one spindly high heel to the other, and adjusted the strap of her leather handbag. "I need your help with my suitcases."

He had the nerve to laugh in her face. "Do I look like a damn bellhop?"

"Ross—"

"You're about to learn another important lesson, Diana."

"Great," she mumbled under her breath. "This must be rule number two."

"Only pack what you can carry."

She planted her hands on her hips and glared at him. "It's a little late for advice, Mr. St. Clair."

"It's never too late for advice, Ms. Winsted," he shot back with what sounded suspiciously like a chuckle.

"But I can't manage all of this luggage by myself."

"Only bring the necessities. Leave the rest here," was his suggestion.

"I can't just abandon my belongings out in the middle of the jungle."

Was the man crazy?

Ross shrugged. "I understand the town of Port Manya is about a mile down the road in that direction," he said, pointing to the east. "There's only one hotel. You shouldn't have any trouble finding it. I wouldn't dawdle, however. It will be dark in another half hour."

Surely he wasn't going to desert her. Not when he'd been so kind on the airplane, offering her coffee, keeping an eye on her while she slept, even saving some of his lunch for her to eat.

But she had a feeling that Ross St. Clair was nobody's fool. She shouldn't have kissed him. That was when the trouble had started.

Well, actually, the trouble had started yesterday afternoon when he'd accosted her in the Metro Manila Airport. But who was splitting hairs?

Diana stood there and watched him walk away. She reminded herself to stay calm. He was simply trying to teach her a lesson. "Ross, please—"

He stopped, kicked at a rock in the road and swore fluently in several languages. She knew he was disgusted with her, with himself, with the whole bloody situation.

Ross turned halfway around. "Wait there, Diana. I'll be right back."

With that, he took off across a sugarcane field. There was a boy of ten or eleven working a two-wheeled cart and a team of oxen along the perimeter, collecting what was left after the recent harvest. Ross spoke to the youngster and gestured in her direction. Then he took several coins from his pocket, and the boy nodded, grinning from ear to ear. The two of them headed toward her.

"The kid's name is Pablo. He will deliver your suitcases to the hotel in town. I gave him a few pesos as a down payment, but I promised that the pretty lady would reward him with even more pesos when her bags arrived in good shape and not covered with mud or dung or sugarcane juice.''

She wrinkled her nose at Ross and spoke to the boy. ''Hotel Paraiso?''

''Hotel Paraiso,'' he repeated shyly.

She smiled at him and resisted the urge to ruffle his dark hair with her hand. ''Thank you, Pablo.''

Ross patted the boy's thin shoulders as they loaded the four matching and expensive pieces of Louis Vuitton onto the primitive cart. ''*Salamat,* Pablo.''

''What does *salamat* mean?'' she inquired as they started off along the dirt road, the boy and oxen-drawn conveyance following at a discreet distance behind them.

'' 'Thanks' in Tagalog.''

She looked at him out of the corner of her eye. ''*Salamat,* Ross.''

''*Walang anoman.*'' He translated his response for her, ''You're welcome.''

A quarter of a mile later Diana wished she'd had the sense to bring along walking shoes on this trip. Or, at least, a pair of Reeboks.

Of course, she hadn't realized she would be hiking down a narrow road cut out of the dense jungle while wearing a three-hundred-dollar pair of imported Italian high heels and an even more expensive designer outfit.

She permitted herself a small sigh. What in the world was she doing on this remote island? Why had Yale dragged her out here in the middle of the Pacific Ocean? And where was he, anyway?

This wasn't at all how she'd pictured her reunion with her fiancé. She had envisioned a lovely candlelight dinner in the Manila Hotel, complete with flowers and champagne. Yale would be dressed in a beautifully tailored suit and she in her favorite cocktail dress.

Instead, she was trudging along a dirt path that had ruts the size of craters. She was hot and she was tired. She was hungry and thirsty. She could feel the perspiration dripping down her back. The silk dress was clinging to her skin. Her hair was coming undone from its usually neat chignon. Her feet were killing her.

And the last thing she would get from the silent man beside her was sympathy.

It was nearly dark by the time they reached the outskirts of the town.

Diana took one look at the corrugated tin-roofed shacks, the unpaved streets filled with naked children, clucking chickens and barking dogs, and exclaimed weakly, "This can't be Port Manya. There must be some mistake."

She prayed there was some mistake!

"There's no mistake. This is Port Manya," Ross insisted as he headed for the hotel.

Diana was in shock. Nevertheless, she hurried along behind him, catching a glimpse of a single row of ramshackle businesses among the main street.

"But what would Yale be doing in a village like this?" she speculated aloud.

"Beats me. He's your boyfriend." Ross quickly corrected himself. "Excuse me, your fiancé." He put his head back and studied the sign over the doorway.

"Hotel Paraiso. Hotel Paradise. This is it," he announced. "I'll go inside and see what I can find out about Grimmer. Maybe you'd better stay out here on the verandah and wait for Pablo and the rest of your luggage."

"All right, I'll wait here." Diana tried to brush the dirt and the grime and what appeared to be chicken droppings off a wooden bench. She finally gave up and sat down on the very edge of the seat.

It was twilight, but she could still see the local children as they played "kick the can" with a rusty piece of tin that had no top or bottom to it. Their young voices were raised in squeals of delighted laughter. They shouted to one another as they raced back and forth across the street. They didn't seem to mind the filth and the poverty all around them.

"So, this is Port Manya," Diana mused, fanning herself with her handbag. She thought of a sign she had once seen posted on the outskirts of a small picturesque town in Michigan: Look Her Over—She's Beautiful.

The Hotel Paraiso reminded Ross of a scene out of the classic Humphrey Bogart/Ingrid Bergman film, *Casablanca*. Only the piano in the Hotel Paraiso was out of tune. So was the soprano.

He sauntered up to the bar. It apparently served as the check-in and registration desk, as well. There was a well-thumbed, ink-stained guest book beside the cash register, a pre–Second World War model in brass and mahogany. A dried-up ballpoint pen was chained to it.

"What can I do for you?" inquired the man wiping off the countertop. The finish had been scrubbed away long ago, leaving the bare wood exposed.

Ross tipped his hat. "I'm looking for somebody."

The bartender gave him an inscrutable smile and said philosophically, "We are all looking for someone, or something, are we not?"

Ross rubbed the back of his neck and returned the smile with one of his own. "I suppose we are. But I'm looking for someone in particular. Do you have a man named Yale Grimmer registered here?"

Dark island eyes narrowed slightly. "Are you a friend of his?"

Ross shook his head and answered truthfully, "No. Not particularly."

"You do business with him?"

He shook his head again. "I'm just looking for him. It's . . . personal."

A noncommittal reply came from the man behind the counter, "Maybe this Yale Grimmer you are searching for is staying here—maybe he is not."

Ross reached into his pocket and took out a ten-dollar bill. He placed it on the bar. "How about a drink?"

The bartender's eyes lit up. "Whiskey?"

"Whiskey will be fine."

An unlabeled bottle was taken from beneath the bar, and a shot of amber colored liquid was poured into a small glass. Then it was set in front of Ross.

He pushed the money toward the man. "Thanks. Keep the change."

Ross raised the glass to his lips. In a single gulp, he tossed back the homemade liquor. God, the stuff was raw. It burned all the way down to his belly and brought tears to his eyes.

"Is Yale Grimmer staying here?" he asked a second time.

"A man calling himself Grimmer is registered here," replied the bartender as he quickly pocketed the money. "But I haven't seen him since he checked in yesterday."

"What do you mean?"

"He inquired about renting a boat. I gave him the name of a certain fisherman on the other side of the island who might be willing to accommodate him. He went out shortly after that and has not returned." He kept wiping the counter. "Grimmer must be a popular man. There was somebody else here looking for him this morning."

That took Ross by surprise. "Who?"

"Two men."

"Islanders?"

A shake of his head. "Outsiders."

"What did they look like?"

The man behind the bar seemed to be suffering from selective amnesia. "Strangers."

Ross took another ten from his pocket and slid it onto the counter. "Another whiskey, please."

His glass was refilled.

Miraculously the bartender seemed to recover his memory about the same time. "Both men were big." One hand was raised a good foot or more above his head to show just how big. "Muscular. But their eyes were cold and lifeless, like those of a dead fish. There was a bulge under each of their shirts. I think they were carrying guns.''

''Simon Ha, you information-selling old devil!'' came a voice from the doorway of the Hotel Paraiso.

The newcomer was dressed in a faded uniform with an official-looking patch on the sleeve. The swinging doors closed behind him. He strolled over to the bar and spoke directly to Ross. ''I heard there were more strangers in town. Port Manya has become very popular in the last two days.''

''So it would seem,'' he said carefully.

The official gave Ross a quick but thorough once-over. ''I am Sergeant Charoon Bok, Port Manya's chief of police and town barber. This sly one behind the counter is Simon Ha, the owner of the Hotel Paraiso and village elder.''

''Ross St. Clair.''

''You are an American, are you not?''

''Yes, I am.''

''You were in Santo Tomas recently.''

That brought a raised eyebrow. ''News travels fast.''

Sergeant Bok explained. ''My wife's great-uncle by marriage lives in Santo Tomas. He is an old man named Cebu.''

Ross relaxed and broke into a broad grin. ''Ah, I know Cebu well.''

Charoon Bok extended his hand in friendship; he pumped Ross's arm. ''You did a most wonderful thing in digging a new well for Cebu's village. You saved the people of Santo Tomas.''

"I wouldn't go so far as to say that," Ross protested out of modesty.

"Simon Ha, this is the man who was the savior of my wife's great-uncle's village. He showed them exactly where and how to dig a new well. Now they have all the drinking water they require."

"Ah . . ." said Simon Ha, suitably impressed.

"You were also the best man and the guest of honor at my wife's second cousin's wedding. You are most welcome in Port Manya, Ross St. Clair," said the chief of police and town barber. "We will be happy to assist you in any way we can."

"Thank you, Sergeant Bok."

"I understand you are looking for the man who calls himself Yale Grimmer."

"Yes, I am," he admitted. News really did travel fast in Port Manya!

"I will make discreet inquiries on your behalf. Meanwhile, I must bicycle to the other side of the island. There has been a small disturbance. It is all in the line of duty. But I will return by tomorrow evening."

"I'll speak to you then, if Grimmer has not returned."

"Will you be requiring a room for the night?" inquired Simon Ha.

Ross had almost forgotten. "Yes, I will."

"And the beautiful young American lady I passed on my way in," speculated the sergeant. "She is your—sister?"

Ross glanced toward the swinging doors of the Hotel Paraiso. "She is my—wife."

"Your wife," repeated the man behind the bar.

He was in it up to his neck now. "We're new-lyweds."

"In that case, you must have our honeymoon suite. It also happens to be our best room," claimed Simon Ha, and he flashed Ross another of his inscrutable smiles.

He dug into his pocket. "How much do I owe you?"

"You have already paid for your room," spoke up Charoon Bok. "Has he not, Simon?"

"Indeed," said the hotelier, nodding his head. "Indeed, he has. Here is the key. The honeymoon suite is up the stairs. The last door on the right."

"We haven't eaten. Is there someplace we can get a little dinner?"

"My wife and daughters are preparing the evening meal now. You may eat right here in the hotel. Lola will sing for you."

The soprano smiled at Ross from across the small, threadbare lobby.

"You are most gracious, Simon Ha. Thank you, Sergeant." He bowed politely to the two men and headed back to Diana. Damn, if he didn't have some explaining to do.

Diana had just collected her luggage from Pablo. All four suitcases were neatly stacked on the veran-dah outside the Hotel Paraiso. She opened her hand-bag, gave the boy a fistful of coins and said, *"Salamat."*

He grabbed the money and dashed for his cart and oxen before the pretty lady changed her mind.

Ross stepped out into the twilight. "You won't solve the world's problems that way."

He watched as her back stiffened; she didn't turn around. "Perhaps not."

"You gave him too much."

"I don't care," she said in a softly defiant tone.

"The news will spread like wildfire. Tomorrow there will be a dozen children following you wherever you go."

She stared straight ahead. "I won't mind. I like children."

He looked at her askance.

She turned. "Don't look so surprised, Ross. Didn't you think I would?"

"Frankly, no," he said bluntly.

"Well, it all goes to show how wrong even you can be. I happen to like children very much."

Ross had more important things on his mind, like saving his neck. He took off his khaki hat, punched at the shapeless crown with his fist and jammed it back on his head. "Look, Diana, there has been a glitch in our plans."

"A glitch?"

He cut straight to the heart of the matter. "Grimmer isn't here."

She went very still. There was an unnatural calmness to her voice when she said, "Yale isn't here? I don't understand."

"He arrived yesterday, registered at the hotel and went out to rent a boat from a fisherman. No one has seen him since."

"But I talked to him last night."

"Did he mention where he was calling from?"

"No. We didn't have a good connection, as you know. It was difficult to hear him."

"Did you notice any background noise?"

"You mean other than static? No, I didn't." Her hand went to her mouth; Ross noticed it was shaking. "Do they suspect foul play?"

"Foul play?"

"Has Yale been declared a missing person?"

"Hell, I don't know. All I do know is we're not the only ones looking for him."

A frown creased her brow. "Not the only ones?"

"The owner of the hotel told me there were two men here earlier today asking for your boyfriend."

"Could they be the two men you overheard talking on the beach?" she said after a moment.

"Not from the description I was given." He thought for a second. "But it does match up with a couple of guards I saw with them."

Diana shivered and wrapped her arms around herself despite the warm tropical night. "Something's wrong, Ross. I can feel it."

"A woman's intuition?" he said sardonically. But he had to agree with her. There was something real fishy about this whole damn business.

"What do we do now?"

He broke it down into manageable parts. "Have some dinner. Try to get some sleep. Hope Grimmer turns up by morning."

She glanced at the dingy hotel behind him. "I assume these are the only accommodations in town."

"You assume correctly." Then he added, "By the way, the chief of police was asking about you."

"The chief of police?" she said nervously, fidgeting with the strap of her handbag.

"He was the man in the faded uniform who walked by you a few minutes ago."

"What did you tell him about me?"

"I *didn't* tell him you were engaged to Grimmer."

She looked up into his eyes. "Why not?"

Ross took off his hat again and drove a hand through his damp hair. "I'm not sure I can explain it."

"Try."

"Gut instinct."

"Gut instinct?" Diana raised an elegant eyebrow. "Is that anything like a woman's intuition?"

Touché.

He apprised her of the situation. "I didn't want those two big goons coming back and finding out that Grimmer's fiancée was staying here at the hotel."

For once she didn't argue with him. "Can we get rooms for the night?"

"No."

"No? I thought you just said—"

"Not rooms. One room."

"One room?" Her voice rose a quarter of an octave. "Is that all they have available?"

"I didn't ask."

"Why not?"

"I told Simon Ha and Sergeant Bok that we only needed one room."

"Why would you tell them that?"

Ross held up his hands in front of him. "Now, Diana, I want you to promise me that you won't raise a fuss until we've had our dinner and retire to our room for the night."

"*Our* room?"

"The honeymoon suite."

A faint color rose in her cheeks. "My God, Ross, what have you done?"

"Sergeant Bok asked if you were my sister."

"I hope you informed him to the contrary."

"I did." He took a deep breath and prepared for the worst. "I told him you were my wife."

Seven

"**Y**our wife!" It was two hours later and Diana still wanted to strangle him.

"Look. I'm sorry. It was the best I could do under the circumstances," Ross said, closing the door of the honeymoon suite behind them.

"Why couldn't you simply tell these people the truth?"

He threw his hat down on the bedside table. "I'm not sure I know what the truth is anymore."

Diana paced back and forth in front of him like a caged lioness. "Well, I do. So let me spell it out for you. My name is Diana Winsted. Yours is Ross St. Clair. I am engaged to be married to a businessman named Yale Grimmer." She turned the ring around on her finger and massaged the spot where the diamond had been digging into her palm all day. "I have just flown halfway around the world to join my fiancé. He called last night and asked me to meet him on Port Manya. This morning I caught the first flight out here from Manila. You came along for the ride. Those are the facts. That is the truth."

She was mad. Madder than hell. She had just spent the most uncomfortable evening of her life pretending to be married to Ross St. Clair.

Saint Clair, indeed, according the villagers in this godforsaken backwater town. Ross could do no wrong in their eyes. And all because he'd dug a lousy well for someone's uncle?

"I know the people in this part of the world, Diana. You don't. Theirs is a conservative and deeply religious society. A single woman, even if she is engaged to be married, doesn't travel alone. She is always chaperoned. Whether you like it or not, you need my protection."

"This isn't the Middle Ages," she snapped.

"It may as well be out here. Society's rules haven't changed that much in these isolated cultures. A woman on her own can only be one thing."

She stopped pacing and quirked a perfectly arched brow in his direction. "What, pray tell, is that?"

Ross gave her a long, hard look. "To put it in euphemistic terms, a 'lady of the evening.'"

Her mouth dropped open. "You're kidding."

"I'm not."

"That is the most idiotic, narrow-minded, chauvinistic, outdated—"

Cutting her off, Ross said, "Rant and rave all you want, Diana. That's the way it is. Trust me, pretending we're married will save us both a lot of trouble as long as we're on this island.''

She threw up her hands in frustration and sank down on the edge of the mattress. "How am I supposed to explain to my fiancé that I'm 'married' to another man?''

"If you ask me, your fiancé is the one who should be doing the explaining," Ross said, his voice and manner dry.

He was right, of course. But Diana wasn't about to admit it to him.

She wet her lips with her tongue and drew in a deep breath. "I'm dirty and I'm tired. All I want to do is take a shower and crawl into bed.''

"Don't let me stop you," he said, plunking himself down on a rattan chair that had seen better days. He untied his boots, eased them off his feet and tossed them into the nearest corner. Then he stood and unbuckled his belt.

Diana sprang up. "Just what in the name of heaven do you think you're doing now?''

His head raised. "Undressing?''

"Why?''

"Because I prefer not to sleep in my clothes.''

"You can't stay here.''

"I'm your husband, remember? Where do you suggest I go?''

Diana pointed to the door. "Out.''

"Out where?'' Ross said between his teeth.

He had her. She could hardly order him out of their hotel room when there was no place else to go. "You really are a b—''

"Such language, Ms. Winsted."

"—buckaroo!" she finished.

"We're two mature adults," said Ross in what he no doubt considered a reasonable tone of voice. "I'm sure we can find a way to peacefully coexist for one night."

Diana sniffed. "I'm sure we can, too. If you keep your pants on."

His mouth curved sardonically. "Do you mind if I take them off to shower?"

"Of course not. Don't be ridiculous."

"Do you want to bathe first, or shall I?" he inquired with excruciating politeness.

"You go first. I have some unpacking to do," she informed him, digging around in her handbag for the keys to her luggage.

"Lock the door behind me and don't open it for anyone," Ross instructed as he grabbed a towel and headed down the hall to the communal bathroom.

"Not for anyone?" she called after him.

"Not for anyone but me, sweetheart," came back to her in gritty masculine tones.

Diana was ready for him when Ross returned fifteen minutes later. Her clothes were unpacked and neatly hung in the old-fashioned wardrobe. She'd peeled down to her bra and panties, and slipped into a wrapper that modestly covered her from neck to ankle. She had her nightgown over her arm, shampoo and conditioner grasped in her right hand, toothbrush and a tube of toothpaste in her left. She was ready to do battle.

"Don't forget your towel," he remarked, draping it over her other arm.

"Thanks. Is there anything I should know about operating the shower?"

"Nope. It's your standard cold-and-cold running water."

Her heart sank. "No hot water?"

Ross slanted her a glance. "This isn't exactly the Hilton, Diana."

"I'm well aware of that," she shot back.

"Wait a minute." He dug around in his knapsack and came up with a plastic bottle of Evian. "You'd better brush your teeth with this."

"Bottled water?"

"I've had all of my shots. But it wouldn't hurt for you to take a few extra precautions."

She shuffled her toilet articles around and accepted the peace offering. *"Salamat."*

"Walang anoman."

As she traipsed down the hallway toward the "conveniences," Diana couldn't resist tossing over her shoulder, "Lock the door behind me and don't open it for anyone."

Ross smirked. "Not for anyone?"

"Not for anyone but me, sweetheart," she trailed behind her.

Actually the shower turned out to have cold-and-cold "dripping" water, but at least when she was done Diana felt reasonably clean. She even managed to rinse most of the shampoo out of her hair.

Then she stood for a moment in front of the bathroom mirror and studied her reflection.

"Watch your step, Diana Winsted," she whispered to the vulnerable blonde in the cracked glass. "He's the wrong man for you, and you know it." Then she took a comb to her wet hair and ruthlessly worked through the tangles, the gold charm bracelet on her wrist tinkling with each movement.

When she returned, the door of the honeymoon suite was unlocked. She let herself in. Ross was stretched out on top of the covers on one side of the double bed, a pillow propped up at his back, arms folded behind his head. He was wearing a pair of clean khaki slacks and nothing else.

"I didn't know which side you usually slept on," he said with ominous calm.

Her gaze faltered. "It—it doesn't matter."

He frowned. "I've never seen you with your hair down before."

Diana self-consciously raised a hand to her wet head. "I, ah, washed it."

"I can see that." He added after a moment, "I like it down."

"Thank you."

"You aren't wearing any makeup."

She quickly stowed her toilet articles in her carryon bag. "No."

"You look younger. And prettier."

She swallowed hard and tried to think of something appropriate to say to him in return. She didn't think *you look even more dangerous without your clothes* was it.

Ross sat up and swung his long legs over the edge of the bed. "You hop in. I'll unravel the mosquito netting and turn off the lights."

"Do you think the netting is really necessary?" she inquired, slipping between the sheets.

"You wouldn't ask that question if you'd ever slept out here in the tropics. I swear some nights you think the mosquitoes are the size of hornets. Bloodthirsty devils, too."

Diana decided to take his word for it.

Ross lowered the mosquito netting around the bed and flicked off the light switch. The room was plunged into darkness. Diana felt the mattress give way beside her as he stretched out again.

They were suddenly cocooned in a world of their own. The night mounted around them.

Five minutes passed.

Then ten.

"Diana, are you awake?"

She sighed and answered him. "Yes."

"Are you in love with Yale Grimmer?"

"Ross, please—"

"All it takes is a simple yes or no."

She stared up through the mosquito netting at the ceiling. "It's not that simple."

"Why isn't it?"

She had no intentions of discussing her relationship with Yale, not with Ross St. Clair, not with anyone. She said carefully, "My fiancé and I both know what we want from marriage. We understand each other. We're two of a kind."

"I don't believe that," the man lying beside her said almost savagely.

"It's true."

"You make it sound more like a business merger than a love match. Whatever happened to grand passion between a man and a woman?"

After a long pause, Diana answered with some difficulty, "Perhaps grand passion is overrated."

"I would have agreed with you once. I used to think that what I needed in a wife was the perfect hostess." Ross made a self-deprecating sound. "Now I know better."

Silence filled the room again.

The moon slipped out from behind a bank of clouds, sending a sliver of pale light into the darkness.

Diana watched out of the corner of one eye as Ross turned his head on the pillow and stared at her searchingly. "Don't marry Grimmer, Diana. You'll regret it for the rest of your life."

"I won't have any regrets."

His voice was sharp with tension. "You think you can live without passion?"

"I know I can."

He rolled over onto his side and faced her in the moonlight. "Lady, you're either a liar or a fool."

Suddenly hot tears burned the back of her eyes. His words hurt more than he would ever know.

Diana swallowed and spoke hoarsely. "Passion simply isn't important to me."

"I think it is." Ross moved closer. She could feel his warm breath on her face. "I dare you to kiss me and prove me wrong."

She turned and brushed her cool lips across his cheek. "There."

"Afraid, Diana?"

"Afraid?"

"That wasn't much of a kiss. Are you afraid to find out the truth?"

She accepted his dare. "No."

This time she went up on one elbow and bent over him. She could feel the heat radiating from his body. Her hand brushed against his bare chest, his skin was hot to the touch.

She inhaled deeply. His scent filled her nostrils; it was clean and masculine. He smelled of soap and damp hair and the exotic night.

"Maybe this isn't a good idea."

He disagreed with her. "Trust me, it's a very good idea, sweetheart."

Diana gave herself a quick pep talk. Whatever had happened between Ross and herself on the plane this morning was the result of an overactive imagination, or an acute case of jet lag. Nothing more.

She was about to prove him wrong. Dead wrong. She was simply not interested in, or capable of, grand passion. That's all there was to it.

Diana touched her lips to his and, once again, she burst into flames.

While her first mistake had been kissing him on the airplane that morning, accepting Ross's dare and kissing him in the intimacy of a moonlit bedroom was an even bigger mistake.

Diana realized in an instant that she was in over her head. She was no longer in control of the situation. The still-functioning part of her brain wondered how that could be, she had never once lost control with Yale.

What was it about Ross St. Clair?

Was it the excitement of the unknown? The seductive allure of the forbidden? The thrill of the dangerous? Did she foster some secret desire to be seduced by an untamed, uncivilized male? A soldier of fortune? A cowboy? A man who lived by his brawn instead of his brain?

Ross kissed her, and she forgot everything but the touch of his lips, the taste of his mouth—oh, Lord, she loved the taste of him—the heat of his flesh, the hard muscles of his chest and shoulders as he took her into his arms.

Suddenly there was no Pacific Ocean. No jungle. No Port Manya. No Hotel Paraiso. No dingy bar. No threadbare honeymoon suite with a rickety, squeaky double bed. There was only Ross and the way he made her feel.

It frightened her.

Then she even forgot to be afraid.

He kissed her and she only wanted more. He thrust his tongue between her parted lips, and she chased after it with her own. Her pulse was beating in double time. Then triple. Her heart seemed caught in her throat. She couldn't swallow. She couldn't breathe. She didn't care.

His hands were on her neck, her shoulders, her arms. She could feel his roughened skin, the calluses on his palms, through the material of her wrapper. Her only thought was how good he would feel against her bare skin.

He found her rib cage. He spanned her body with both of his hands. Then he reached up with his thumbs and flicked her nipples through the material of her gown and robe.

Diana's lips opened, and a low, husky groan escaped.

"Yes," was all Ross muttered.

The wrapper was pushed aside, her nightgown followed, and she could feel the moist heat of his mouth on her, the hard tip of his tongue tracing a wild erotic pattern back and forth across the rigid tip of her breast. The serrated edges of his teeth gently nipped her. His tongue lathed her. His lips caressed her. Then he drew her deeper and deeper into his mouth until she thought he intended to swallow her whole.

Passion.

The word was forevermore burned into every cell of Diana's brain, every nerve ending of her body, every inch of her flesh. This was passion in its primitive, all-consuming form. It was a fever in the mind, in the body, in the soul.

His first mistake had been kissing her on the airplane that morning. Now he couldn't seem to get enough of her. It was the damnedest thing.

Diana was everything he had imagined she might be, could be, and more, realized Ross as he covered her breast with his mouth. The first time he had set eyes on her he'd asked himself if there beat the heart of a passionate and sensuous woman beneath the cool, haughty exterior.

He had his answer.

She was like wildfire in his arms. His blood ran hot and heavy in response.

He could feel the heat pouring from her. He knew her skin must be flushed with sexual excitement, her body soft and moist and ready for him. She was aroused, and the realization only aroused him all the more.

He yearned to strip the bedclothes from her and ease her lovely thighs apart. He wanted desperately to unzip his suddenly too-tight and uncomfortable pants, release his rigid flesh and bury himself in her right up to the hilt.

He dreamed of watching her face as he thrust into her again and again, as he brought her to a shattering climax, as he emptied himself into her utterly and completely.

A short, succinct expletive exploded in his brain.

He groaned aloud, "I can't!"

Diana drew back and stared at him with passion-glazed eyes. "You can't?" she repeated, obviously at a loss to understand what he meant.

"We can't," he bit off sharply.

"Can't what?"

"We can't let this go any further than it has," Ross stated in a tightly controlled voice. He rolled over onto his back and gave a short, self-mocking laugh. "Some Boy Scout I'd make. I'm not even prepared."

The woman beside him silently adjusted her night-gown and wrapper.

"I'm sorry, Diana."

"It—it wasn't your fault," she whispered.

"Yes, it was." Ross punched the pillow behind his head with a hard fist. "I shouldn't have started what I wasn't prepared to finish."

In a small but firm voice Diana repeated, "We're only human, flesh and blood. We got a little carried away. We went a little crazy. It happens. That's what you said this morning."

He felt like a grizzly bear with a burr caught in its paw. In short, he felt like hell. "Yeah, well, maybe I lied," he growled.

She apparently hadn't thought of that. "Did you lie to me, Ross?"

A tense frown bracketed his mouth. "No." He reached over and took her hand in his. It was ice-cold. So was the bracelet on her wrist. "I didn't lie to you, Diana. I never have. I never will. I promise."

After a minute or two, she went so far as to admit, "You were right, you know."

"About what?"

"I'm a fool and a liar."

"You're no fool, sweetheart. And we all lie to ourselves once in a while. It's a natural part of self-preservation."

"I thought I could live without passion." Her voice caught. "I was wrong."

Ross turned his head. He could clearly see her profile in the moonlight, and the tears poised on her eyelids. "Didn't you ever feel this way with Grimmer?"

She swallowed. "No."

"Oh, hell..."

"What?"

"I'd better get out of here before I do something we'll both regret."

"I don't understand."

Ross took her hand and placed it on the hard bulge below his waist. "Feel that?"

She flinched. "Yes."

"You know what it is, don't you?"

He heard her gulp. "Of course I do."

He made a half angry, half helpless sound. "Well, damned if I can explain it, but I want you, Diana Winsted, more than I have ever wanted any woman."

She gave a soft, "Oh..."

"If I stay here, we're going to end up making love. And frankly, sweetheart, neither of us is prepared for that." Ross pushed the mosquito netting aside for a moment and swung out of bed.

"Where are you going?"

He grabbed his shirt. "Out."

"Out where?"

He shrugged and quickly pulled on his boots.

"But you said there was no place to go."

"I can always take another cold shower," he said, his voice a harsh rumble.

"Ross?" It was a little cry for help.

He made himself walk away from her. Someday she'd thank him.

One last command was issued. "Lock the door behind me, Diana."

Ross stalked down the hallway, took the stairs two at a time and made it to the verandah of the Hotel Paraiso before he managed another breath.

Like a litany it kept going around and around in his head: *Let your conscience be your guide, Ross. Let your conscience be your guide.*

There was a rusty tin can lying in the middle of the street. He gave it a good kick with his boot.

Eight

Diana lay there in the dark and fought back the tears. She didn't blame Ross. It was as much her fault as his. If you were foolish enough to play with fire, you always took the chance of getting burned. That basic rule applied in any part of the world.

Ross had set out to teach her a lesson tonight, and, in the end, he had done her a favor. She'd learned something important about herself: she was not an "ice princess." She was not a coldhearted bitch. She did not have a lump of black coal where her heart was supposed to be. She was not frigid, as the few men she had dated since college had claimed.

She was a warm, responsive woman—with the right man.

Surely, if she could feel such overwhelming passion

with Ross St. Clair, there was nothing very wrong with her and something very right about her.

Suddenly Diana was feeling almost cheerful. She fluffed her pillow, straightened the bed covers and made herself as comfortable as possible on the lumpy, too-soft mattress. Then she stretched out and waited for Ross to return.

It gave her time to think.

Yale Grimmer.

Tall. Handsome. Well educated. Ambitious. Polite. Well mannered. Safe.

It occurred to Diana that one of Yale's greatest attractions for her—besides his impeccable credentials, of course—was the fact that he had never pressed for physical intimacy. His kisses were pleasant and nonthreatening. He was gentle. He was thoughtful. He was as concerned for her feelings as much as his own. He never lost control.

He was, in short, the perfect gentleman.

It was just that she was no longer certain she wanted to marry the perfect gentleman.

Maybe she had suspected all along that there was something vital missing between Yale and herself. Now, thanks to Ross St. Clair, she knew what it was: passion.

Diana rolled over and faced the empty side of the bed. She reached out and ran her hand along the sheets where Ross had lain, the indentation in the pillow where his head had been. She inhaled, and the distinctive, masculine scent of him that clung to the bed covers filled her senses.

If she were honest with herself—and it was long overdue—she had tasted passion and she liked it. It was intoxicating. It was addictive. It was as necessary to her now as the air she breathed or the food she ate.

She wasn't naive enough to believe that passion by itself was enough to ensure eternal happiness. But she knew that it was absolutely essential between a man and a woman, that it was the foundation upon which a relationship was built.

Ross had given her a rare and precious gift tonight: he had shown her the truth about herself. She had learned a valuable lesson. He had been an excellent teacher. She wanted to tell him *salamat*.

Diana curled up and pulled the covers over her. She tried to stay awake, but the long days of travel were catching up with her again, and her eyelids grew heavy.

What had Ross instructed her to do as he'd stormed out of their room?

She couldn't seem to remember.

As her eyes closed, a question crossed her drowsy mind: had she locked the door?

Diana wasn't sure what awakened her. She pushed herself up onto her elbows and stared into the inky darkness of the honeymoon suite.

It was the click of the doorknob that brought her straight up in bed. It also reminded her that she had forgotten to lock the door.

Her next thought was reassuring. It had to be Ross returning to their room. Who else could it be? Only a handful of local residents even knew that "Mr. and Mrs. St. Clair" were staying at the Hotel Paraiso.

Of course, in a village the size of Port Manya, what one person knew, everyone knew, right down to the deaf octogenarian rocking on his front porch and the smallest child playing in the street. News traveled fast here. No doubt because there was so little of it. The arrival of a stranger was a major event. In which case, she and Ross should provide enough gossip to last for months, possibly for years.

The tarnished brass knob turned. The door opened an inch or two on its squeaky hinges.

"Ross, is that you?" she called out quietly, peering through the mosquito netting.

There was no answer.

The door was cracked open another inch.

"Ross?"

There was still no response.

Diana wasn't in the mood for games. Not at this time of the night. "If you're trying to frighten me, you're not succeeding," she said in a censorious tone.

There was the soft thud of a footstep, then another.

She tried a different tact. "Yale?"

Just as the door to the honeymoon suite swung open wide enough for a man to pass through, the moon slipped behind a cloud. The room was plunged into darkness.

Diana couldn't explain how, but she suddenly knew that something was wrong. Dreadfully wrong. It wasn't Yale at the door. And it certainly wasn't Ross. She would know if it were Ross.

The moon broke away from the bank of clouds. A pale yellow light illuminated the bedroom. There were two shadows looming in the open doorway.

Her hand flew to her mouth. She barely managed to stifle the startled gasp that sprang to her lips. She wanted to scream. Instead, she bit down hard into the soft flesh between her thumb and forefinger, and tried to think.

What to do? God in heaven, what should she do?

From what she could determine the midnight intruders matched the description of the two men Ross had told her were looking for Yale earlier that day. They were both tall and thick through the shoulders. They had no necks. They bulged like muscle men.

They looked like thugs.

"She's got to be here somewhere," one of them whispered.

"Think Grimmer's with her?"

"Don't know. But Carlos said to bring them both back alive, along with the merchandise."

"Then don't use your gun unless you have to, stupid," hissed the other one.

Gun?

They had guns!

Diana's heart began to slam against her chest. All she could hear was its violent drumming in her ear. She had to stay calm. She had to think fast. Could she slip under the bed before they discovered her presence? Or would that be the first place they'd search once they found the empty, rumpled bed covers?

It was too far to the closet. There was no place to hide. And they were between her and the door.

She was trapped.

Diana Winsted understood for the first time what it was to fear for her life. It wasn't something she'd ever thought about, considered, imagined, dreamed of. Not even in her worst nightmares.

Hers had been a sheltered, privileged existence surrounded by loving parents and grandparents, an adoring younger brother, numerous friends and devoted sorority sisters. Disappointments had been few and far between. She didn't take her good fortune for granted, but she hadn't appreciated the simple fact of being, feeling, *safe.*

She was genuinely afraid now. She didn't know what to do, but she hated the feeling of helplessness that accompanied it. She regretted not taking a course in self-defense. She wished she had a gun. She wished she knew how to use a gun.

Where was Ross?

She needed him more than ever. He would know what to do. After all, he was the expert at these things. She was willing to bet that he wouldn't cower in the corner of his bed while two gorillas sneaked into his hotel room.

Diana realized she had only one weapon at her disposal. She decided she'd better use it.

Opening her mouth, she yelled at the top of her lungs, *"Ross! Help me! Ross!"*

"She's here somewhere and screaming loud enough to wake the dead," complained one of the thugs as they bumped into each other in the ensuing confusion.

"Well, find her and shut her up."

"You find her and shut her up."

"Ross! Help! Someone Help!" Diana kept up the racket as long as she could, only pausing for a split second to catch her breath. *"Ross! Help! Ross!"*

"Who the hell's Ross?"

"How should I know? Do I look like a damn mind reader?" growled one of the muscle men.

"There she is in the bed. Grab her."

One of them dove for her. Diana quickly scampered to the opposite side of the mattress. She tried to blind the man with a faceful of mosquito netting. When that failed, she grabbed a pillow and began to hit him with all her might.

Damn, her nightgown and wrapper were proving to be more of a hindrance than a help. She wished she wore pajamas to sleep in. At least they would have facilitated movement more easily.

The second thug came up behind her. Diana spun around and kicked out with her bare foot, trying to connect with his groin. She remembered reading somewhere that it was best to go for the attacking male's physical weaknesses: the groin, the eyes, the throat, a stiletto-sharp high heel ground into his instep.

Too bad her three-hundred-dollar pair of imported Italian high heels were neatly lined up in the closet across the room. They would have finally come in handy.

Then one of the men succeeded in grabbing Diana by the arm. She fought like a tigress, like a wild creature that refused to be caged. She rolled into a ball, opened her mouth and sank her teeth into his skin.

He jumped back, holding his injured hand, and complained to his accomplice. "Ouch! The bitch bit me!"

"Stop your bellyaching."

"I'm not bellyaching. But it hurts."

"Don't be such a damn crybaby."

Diana waited for the right moment and prayed that Lady Luck would be with her.

She was.

The moon slipped behind a veil of clouds and Diana knew it was her last and best chance to escape. She pushed the mosquito netting aside, jumped off the foot of the bed and made a mad dash for the open door.

"Quick! Grab her! She's making a run for it!"

Diana hitched up her nightgown, raced through the doorway and out into the hall. She flew down the stairs, nearly tripping on the hem of her gown. Her wrapper came loose. She shrugged it off her shoulders, letting it fall into a silky heap behind her, hoping that one of her pursuers would slip on it like a banana peel and end up flat on his back.

Like a shot, she was across the lobby and out the front door of the Hotel Paraiso. She hit the street in a single bound and sprinted as fast as her bare feet would carry her, never daring to look back, not caring that her heart was about to burst in her chest.

She ran and she ran and she ran until she hit a solid wall of human flesh.

"Diana!"

Ross! Ohmigod, it was Ross!

Her breath was coming in great gulps. She couldn't speak. Not a word. Not even his name. But he immediately realized she wasn't out for a casual evening stroll.

Ross quickly drew her into the shadows and lightly covered her mouth with his hand. Then he pulled her down behind a corrugated box, and they watched together as the two thugs barreled out the front door of the hotel and stood there staring up and down the deserted street.

One of them kicked the railing of the verandah and bit off a brief expletive. "We've lost her."

"The boss isn't going to like this."

"That's for damn sure."

The second thug was still massaging his injured hand where Diana had sunk her teeth into him. "He didn't warn us she was a hellcat."

"Maybe he didn't know."

"Now what do we do?"

"Go back to the camp and wait until daylight. We'll never find her in the dark."

"I think my hand's bleeding," whined the wounded gorilla.

"Ah, shut up!" snapped his companion.

"But it's my trigger finger."

"Big deal. You never could shoot straight, anyway."

The two men were still arguing as they took off down the main street of Port Manya. A few minutes later they disappeared from sight.

Diana attempted to speak.

Ross raised his finger to his lips. "Shh..."

Five minutes passed.

Ten.

Fifteen.

Finally he straightened, and Diana attempted to stand up alongside him. Her legs were still shaking. Her knees gave way beneath her weight. Without a word, Ross took her into his arms and held her. He held her close. He held her as if he would never let her go.

She finally stopped trembling.

His face was only an inch from hers. He whispered against her mouth, "Are you all right now?"

She nodded.

"We'll carefully make our way back to the hotel, but stick to the shadows. Understand?"

She nodded her head again.

They moved from shadow to shadow until they reached the bottom step of the verandah. Then they made a dash for the open door. Ross closed it after them and flattened himself against the wall, pulling Diana behind him as though he would shield her with his body if necessary.

He peered around a corner of the window, then announced, "I think they're gone for now."

"For now?"

"They'll be back," he said in dead earnest.

"When?"

"You heard them. Daylight."

Diana was scared stiff. "What will we do?"

"You—*we*—have to get out of here tonight."

"Where will we go?"

Ross shook his head. "I don't know yet. We've got a few things to take care of first."

"What things?"

"I'll explain while you pack." He hustled her back up the flight of stairs to the honeymoon suite.

They paused in the doorway. The mosquito netting was in a torn heap on the floor. The pillows and bed covers were strewn haphazardly about the room, and the mattress was half off the bed.

"Looks like you put up quite a fight," commented Ross.

"I tried. The odds were against me, of course. It was two to one."

"What did you do to the guy who complained he was bleeding?"

Diana's eyes blazed. "I bit him."

Ross cleared his throat. "Pack one small bag. Take only what is absolutely necessary." His face was drawn in deep lines of concentration. "I'm going downstairs to find Simon Ha."

"Simon Ha?"

"I'll need something to barter with for food and water."

Diana quickly dumped her jewelry out onto the dresser. She picked out several rings, a pair of gold hoops, a brooch done in semiprecious stones.

"What about this?" suggested Ross, indicating the gold charm bracelet on her wrist.

"No. Not that. It was a birthday present from Yale. He would never forgive me if I sold it."

Ross shrugged and opened the closet door. He began to rifle through her expensive designer dresses, picking out one or two in the brightest colors and a pair of flashy high heels.

"What are you doing with my clothes?"

"I need something to trade with Lola."

"Lola?"

He turned and eyed her from head to toe. "You need a pair of sensible walking shoes and something practical to wear. There isn't a damn thing in this closet that will be useful to you where we're going."

"But that dress cost me five hundred dollars," she softly wailed as he yanked it from the hanger.

Ross speared her with his eyes. "How much is your life worth to you, Diana?"

She snapped her mouth shut. "Take this one, as well. It's a good color for Lola," she said, grabbing another expensive outfit from the wardrobe.

Arms full, Ross paused in the doorway. "This time keep the door locked. I'll be back in a half hour. Maybe less. Be ready to put on the clothes I bring you. And remember only pack what you can carry."

"Right."

"You'd better bring the rest of your jewelry. We may need it to barter for food and supplies, depending on how long we're out there."

Diana didn't want to ask, but, in the end, she did, "Out *where?*"

"We're on the run, baby."

"The run?"

"We're heading into the jungle."

Nine

They'd been on the run all night, and Diana hadn't complained once. Not a word. Not a sigh. Not a gripe or a grumble. Not a moan or groan of self-pity.

Ross was amazed.

She had to be hot, or tired, or hungry. Probably all three. He knew he was.

The strap of her carryon bag was digging into her shoulder; he could tell by the way she shifted the weight from one arm to the other every now and then.

Her feet must hurt. Her legs must ache. Every muscle in her body must be screaming for relief. He was pushing her harder than she had ever been pushed before in her entire life. Yet she was keeping up with him, and without a word of complaint.

He turned his head and said just loud enough to be heard, "How are you doing?"

"Fine."

"How do the boots feel?"

"Fine."

Lola, the singer and sometime barmaid at the Hotel Paraiso, hadn't owned any suitable walking shoes, so he'd had to barter for a pair of men's work boots from Simon Ha. One of the few pair on the island, according to the hotelier, since most residents of Port Manya went barefoot.

"They are genuine leather," Simon had claimed as he drove up the already exorbitant asking price. "Excellent workmanship. Brought all the way from Mindanao by my eldest son."

Ross had taken the boots. He'd had no choice.

They weren't an exact fit—there was an inch or two of old newspaper stuffed into the toe of each one—but they sure beat the alternative: Diana's skimpy three-inch-high imported Italian heels.

Lola had been more than willing to trade a blouse, a jacket and a pair of faded jeans for the designer dresses. Of course, the singer was barely five feet tall. Consequently the jeans hit Diana about midcalf. The difference had to be made up with a pair of Ross's socks that reached well above her knees. You didn't go into the jungle at night with bare legs, with bare skin, with bare anything. Not if you were smart.

Ross hadn't explained why.

Diana had wisely *not* asked. There were times when ignorance was bliss.

He wasn't particularly eager to go into details about the necklace-length centipedes; the ants as long as a man's finger; the poisonous spiders; the snakes, especially the giant pythons and the cobras; the *pagil,* a species of jungle boar with a nasty temper; or the purported fifty-six varieties of bats that inhabited the caves on some of these islands. Not to mention the countless nameless creatures that slithered along the jungle floor, and the mosquitoes that could eat you alive.

While they were having dinner together at the Manila Hotel, Ross remembered warning Diana that if she stayed in this part of the world, the veneer of civilization would be stripped away and she would be exposed for who and what she was. It happened to everyone sooner or later.

Perhaps what he was seeing now was the real Diana Winsted. She wore no makeup. Her hair was pulled back into a single utilitarian ponytail, and there was an old Detroit Tigers baseball cap pulled down over her eyes.

She'd caught a glimpse of herself in the mirror as they left the honeymoon suite earlier that night. Much to Ross's astonishment, she had shown no reaction. She hadn't said a solitary word, just turned and walked out the door.

Maybe he had been wrong about her. Maybe he had misjudged her. Maybe Diana wasn't the silly, helpless, useless debutante he had dubbed her in the beginning.

Maybe she was more than just another pretty face and a great pair of legs.

She was turning out to be a good sport. A genuine trouper. A fierce fighter. In fact, one hell of a woman.

She had managed to outwit and escape from the two gorillas who had attacked her in their hotel room.

Ross still blamed himself for that fiasco. He should have known the hired henchmen looking for Yale Grimmer would have a description of Diana, too.

She stuck out like a sore thumb.

How many young, beautiful blondes were there on Port Manya?

But, dammit, last night had been untenable! He had found himself wanting to make love to a woman he couldn't stand. A woman he despised. A woman who drove him crazy. A woman who was engaged to marry another man. A woman he wanted so goddamn much he could literally taste his own desire!

Diana Winsted had become an itch that he desperately needed to scratch. ·

At first, Ross assumed it was the simple fact that he had been celibate for so long. After all, sex had been out of the question for months. He'd been in and out of one hellhole after another. He had seen poverty, disease and despair. He had seen things that made him sick, that made him weep, that made him mad.

He had also been warmly welcomed by kind, gentle, generous people who knew nothing about him, who asked no questions and expected no answers. He had learned their languages, honored their customs and kept to himself.

For the past six months he had been on a quest, a quest to find out what kind of man he was, a quest for self-understanding, self-knowledge, wisdom. He had not been interested in proving his sexual prowess.

Until now.

Ross glanced back at the woman trudging along behind him. "Do you want to stop and rest for five minutes?"

Diana lifted her chin. Her eyes were hidden beneath the brim of the baseball cap, but there was a steely determination in her voice. "How long until dawn?"

"An hour. Maybe less."

"Do you think those two men will follow us as soon as it's daylight?"

He wasn't going to lie to her. "Yes."

"Will they be able to track us?"

"Probably."

"How far is it to Simon's hideout?"

"Another couple of miles. But it will be rough going."

"No."

"No?"

"I don't want to stop for a rest."

They kept going.

The dark of night was gradually replaced by the gray light of dawn. An early-morning mist hung over the jungle, giving it a surreal appearance. There was that one hushed moment between night and day, a time of utter peace and quiet.

The two of them paused and took it in. Neither spoke.

They passed a rushing waterfall, held their kerchiefs under the cool water and retied them around their necks.

Soon after, the rains came. They were both soaked to the skin in less than a minute. Hell, it made no difference; they were already drenched with perspiration.

The rain stopped. The sun came out, and the steam rose from the jungle floor.

Ross stopped and took his bearings. "We're nearly there."

"How can you tell?"

"Simon said, 'go past the first waterfall, the mangrove swamp with its hundreds of varieties of flowers—'" he indicated the brakish waterhole behind them filled with rare and exotic orchids "'—to the wild banana grove. From there you will see the tall forest of *lauan,* also called Philippine mahogany, in front of you. Go straight into the forest for sixty paces and you will see a tree trunk bearing my mark. Then you will know that you are there.'"

"Did Simon Ha draw you a map?"

"Nope."

"Then how—?"

Ross pointed to his forehead. "I can see it clearly. It's all up here."

"I'm impressed." Apparently Diana wasn't being entirely facetious. "Another of your engineering skills?"

"Partly."

The path widened. Side by side they made their way toward the forest of *lauan* trees.

"How did Simon come to learn of this hideout?" Diana inquired as they hiked along.

Ross untied the kerchief from around his neck and mopped his brow. "Apparently it's been a carefully guarded village secret for many years."

"How many years?

"The family of Simon Ha and a number of others hid here from the enemy during the Second World War when their troops landed briefly on Port Manya."

Her eyes grew round as saucers. "But that would have been nearly fifty years ago."

Ross nodded his head. "Even before that, Simon said the villagers used the forest to conceal their wives and daughters whenever pirates stopped on the island to replenish their supplies of food and water."

"They hid their women from the marauders."

"Exactly."

"How does Simon know the hideout is still here?"

Ross began to silently count the number of paces into the trees. "The villagers consider it a sacred trust. Twice a year a small expedition journeys here to pray to the forest gods and make whatever repairs are necessary."

"That is an absolutely amazing story."

"But a true one."

Golden brown eyes were turned on him, and a voice filled with conviction said, "But a true one."

"Fifty-eight. Fifty-nine. Sixty." Ross stopped in the center of a small clearing and announced, "We're here."

Diana spun around in a circle. "But where? I don't see any hideout."

"It wouldn't be much of a hideout if you could," Ross shot back, his tanned face dissolving into a smile.

"There's nothing here but trees. Are you sure you have the right place?"

Ross took Diana gently by the elbow and guided her to one huge specimen in particular. The tree measured a good five feet in diameter and soared one hundred feet and more into the forest canopy overhead. There was a barely discernible notch carved into the bark.

"Simon's mark."

"Simon's mark," she repeated, reaching out to trace it with her fingertip.

Ross dropped his knapsack to the forest floor and took out a length of thick, sturdy rope. He tied one end securely around his waist and made a large loop with the other.

"What are you doing?"

"I'll have to go first. Once I've reached the hideout, I'll lower the hemp ladder so you can climb up."

"Climb up?"

Ross frowned and inquired, "You aren't afraid of heights, are you?"

"No."

"That's good."

Diana put her hand out and placed it lightly on his arm. "Ross, exactly where is Simon's hideout?"

"Didn't I tell you?"

"No, you didn't."

He put his head back and gazed up into the treetops. "It's up there, sweetheart. Up where the trees meet the sky."

Ten

"It's a tree house," Diana exclaimed as they stood on the sturdy wooden platform built among the thick *lauan* branches that were bigger around than a man.

Ross hoisted his knapsack from the forest floor below. It was the last of their belongings and supplies to be transported to the hideout. "I guess you could call it that."

Diana carefully peered over a leafy railing. "But you can't see a thing from down there."

Untying the canvas knapsack, Ross began to loop the length of rope into a coil. "Camouflage—that's the whole idea."

"This place is like something out of *Swiss Family Robinson*," she said with great delight, forgetting for a moment the danger that had driven the two of them out into the night and toward this jungle sanctuary.

"I doubt if the islanders who originally built the hideout had ever read Wyss's book," he observed.

"Probably not."

But it didn't matter. Diana was determined to enjoy this rare glimpse of a wondrous world she had never seen before—and would, undoubtedly, never see again.

"Look, Ross," she whispered, pointing out a brilliantly colored exotic bird that had flown down to perch on a nearby tree limb. She could almost reach out and touch it.

"Kind of makes you feel like Adam and Eve, doesn't it?" he said with a crooked smile. "Or maybe Tarzan and Jane would be more apropos." Then he was all business again. "Let's take an inventory of what we've got available to us up here and make our plans accordingly."

Despite a weariness that went right down to her bones, Diana gave him a crisp salute, snapped the heels of her too-large boots together and, with a "yessir," followed Ross on an inspection of the facilities.

"One thatched-roof sleeping hut," he said, ducking his head and stepping momentarily into the small shelter. "Mats woven from the leaves of the buri palm. Spears and fishing rods made from the *palma brava*. Two *tambô* grass brooms." He turned and handed one to her.

Diana stared at it. "What's this for?"

"Sweeping."

"Sweeping?"

"As in cleaning out any critters that might be taking a nap in our sleeping hut."

A shiver raced down her spine, but Diana replied, "Right. Cleaning out critters."

Ross went down on his haunches and examined a stack of metal boxes neatly piled in one corner of the shelter. He flipped open a lid. "American army rations."

She peered over one of his shoulders. "American army rations here?"

"Black market," he told her by way of an explanation. "Not exactly gourmet dining, but certainly edible." Ross snapped the box shut again.

They found an amazing assortment of other devices in the treetop hideout, including a chamber pot behind a bamboo privacy screen and a makeshift shower rigged up under a contraption that collected rain water.

"All the comforts of home," Ross said as they finished their tour.

Only it wasn't home, of course, Diana thought with sober realization. They weren't playing Tarzan of the jungle and Jane for the fun of it. This wasn't a game. The men who had tried to kidnap her in their hotel room last night had meant business. Serious business.

Life-and-death business.

Diana took off the baseball cap and wiped the perspiration from her face with her sleeve. "How long do you suppose it will take those men to find us?"

"Long enough."

"Long enough for what?"

"For me to create a diversion or two, leave a surprise here and there, set a few mousetraps."

She frowned. "Mousetraps?"

"Maybe rattraps is more like it." Ross's eyes hardened. "If we're lucky, very lucky, maybe we'll catch ourselves a couple of big rats."

Diana reached out and placed her hand on his arm. "You won't take any unnecessary chances, will you?"

Ross tipped her chin up, bent over and brushed his lips across hers. "Of course not. But thanks for being concerned." Then he was all business again. "I've got one more job for you while I'm gone."

"While you're gone?"

"While I'm down below planning a few surprises for our visitors."

"Surprises as in booby traps," she said composedly.

"Exactly."

"What's the job you want me to do?"

Ross dug into his knapsack, took out a vial of yellowish liquid and handed it to her. "I want you to sprinkle this around the perimeter of the hideout—the platform, the hut, the shower, the railing. Everywhere."

"What is it?"

"I don't know the scientific name—if it even has one—but basically it smells like a mongoose."

Diana wrinkled up her nose. "Smells like a mongoose to whom?"

Ross hesitated. "Not to *whom*. To *what*."

She held the vial up to the sunlight. "Okay, it smells like a mongoose to *what?*"

"Snakes."

"Snakes!"

He caught the vial just as it slipped from her hands. "I'm sorry, honey, I should have explained before I gave it to you. How do you feel about snakes?"

Diana gave him a dirty look. "Do you mean the small common variety of garter snake, or the forty-foot-long anaconda?"

He was obviously trying to reassure her. "There aren't any anacondas in this region. They're only found in tropical South America, usually in the Amazon."

"I assume that's the good news."

"There are, however, giant pythons and cobras on these islands."

"That must be the bad news," she said dryly.

Ross continued in a no-nonsense tone of voice, "Most snakes don't like the mongoose. It's their natural enemy."

"Like in Rudyard Kipling's story about Rikki-Tikki-Tavi."

He snapped his fingers. "Now you've got it."

She sighed dramatically. "Why can you never find a good mongoose when you need one?"

He shrugged. "That's why I want you to sprinkle essence of mongoose around to create a barrier."

Diana took the vial from Ross's hand and assured him, "I'll be thorough. Trust me."

"You might rustle up some dinner when you're finished."

She turned a slightly reproachful gaze on him. "I hope you don't mean that literally."

Ross actually laughed out loud. "Try the army rations." He began to gather up his paraphernalia: several coils of rope, a spear, a ball of thin wire, a lethal-looking knife the size of a small machete and sundry odds and ends. "There should be plenty of rainwater in the barrel, if you decide to take a shower." He raised his head and squinted up at the bright sunlight filtering through the treetops. "This might be the perfect opportunity to dry your clothes."

"I'll bet I look a sight," she offered, chuckling good-naturedly.

"You've never looked more beautiful to me," Ross claimed in a husky voice.

Diana's throat constricted. "You won't be gone too long, will you?"

"Not any longer than I have to be, believe me." His voice grew softer; he was almost caressing her with his words. "We both need some food and some sleep, in that order. But I'll rest a whole lot easier once I take care of a few things down below."

She took a step toward him. "Ross, about last night—"

His eyes darkened. "We'll talk when I get back, Diana. I've got something I want to say to you, too."

She put her hands on his shoulders, went up on her tiptoes and pressed a kiss to his mouth. "Watch your back, cowboy."

"I will."

"Promise?"

"I promise." He started down the hemp ladder. "Pull the ladder up once I reach the ground. Don't lower it again until I signal."

"What's the signal?"

"I'll give a whistle."

She peered over the platform at him. "What kind of whistle?"

He winked at her. "A wolf whistle, naturally."

When the whistle came, Diana lowered the ladder and Ross climbed up. It was a toss-up between hunger and exhaustion for both of them. They ate in silence and immediately stretched out on mats in the thatched-roof hut. Sleep came in a matter of a minute, maybe two.

It was the heat of the day. Nothing was active. Even the animals of the forest knew better than to move around in the sultry oven that was the jungle at midday.

Later Diana awakened to stars overhead and a moon on the rise and wondered how that could be. Then she realized there was a trapdoor, a kind of sunroof, in the ceiling of the hut. Ross must have opened it while she slept.

There was a slight breeze cooling her skin as she lay there. The scent of exotic tropical flowers was heavy in the air: blooming vines with names she could not remember. But one. The *cadena de amor.* The "chain of love."

She turned her head and discovered that she was alone in the sleeping hut. Quietly moving to the door, she peered out into the night. At first she couldn't see Ross anywhere. Then there was a slight movement on the other side of the platform, and she knew it was him.

She deliberately left her boots behind and crossed to him in her stocking feet. She made no sound on the wooden floorboards, and was almost directly behind him before she said his name.

"Ross..." She saw him start as he jerked around.

"I thought you were still asleep," he said softly, in nearly a whisper.

"I was until a minute ago." She looked out at the night. "Have you seen anything?"

"Nothing."

"Was it too hot for you to sleep?" From all appearances he was wearing only a pair of khaki pants, and his skin seemed to glisten with perspiration in the moonlight.

"I'm used to the heat."

But Diana noticed he did not answer her question.

She reached out and touched his arm, and she could feel the tension in him like a tautly drawn wire about to snap. "Are you worried about the two men?"

He shook his head and said in a cold, uncompromising voice, "Assuming those two goons ever make it this far, I've taken care of things."

She was still concerned. There was something wrong with Ross—or at least not quite right. Something was on his mind. She could tell.

"Do you want to talk about it?"

He continued to stare straight ahead into the forest canopy. "Talk about what?"

"Whatever it is that's bothering you."

"No."

She didn't understand. "No?"

He uttered a growling profanity. "No, dammit, I don't want to talk about it."

Diana bit her lip.

Then Ross turned and, driving his fingers through his hair in frustration, softly raged, "Don't you get it even yet? Don't you understand?"

She shook her head.

"It's you. You're what's bothering me." His eyes burned into hers. "I don't understand it. I can't explain it. But I want you, Diana."

Her mouth formed his name. She blurted out, "I want you, too."

"Are you sure?"

The question required a simple yes or no. "Yes."

Ross leaned back against a thick branch of the great towering tree and folded his arms across his bare chest; his muscles seemed to strain at the very confines of his skin. It was a minute, maybe longer, before he said, "You're engaged to marry another man."

She looked right at him. "Yale doesn't make me feel the way you do."

"Has he ever tried?"

She swallowed hard. "No."

"Have you wanted him to?"

She shook her head again.

"I told you last night that I wasn't prepared to make love to you," he rasped.

Her eyes grew huge. "Because you don't want me enough?"

A muscle in his face started to twitch. His eyes shimmered fiercely. "I vowed I'd never lie to you. I won't start now. I was telling you the truth last night when I said I wanted you more than I've ever wanted any woman. I desire you, Diana Winsted. I want to make love to you, to be a part of you, to bury myself so deep inside you that we can't tell where I end and you begin. I want to feel your body close tightly around me as you climax again and again and again."

She said in a whisper, "I'm not sure I can."

He went very still. "What?"

She didn't know if she could say it. "Have a climax."

Ross looked at her as if she was crazy. "What in the hell are you talking about?"

Tears welled up at the edge of her eyelids. "I was called an ice princess all the way through high school and college. You can't imagine what that was like." Her eyes drained of vitality. "It wasn't entirely as a result of my appearance. If a guy tried to touch me, I froze. It was awful. Some of my dates thought I was a tease, that I was leading them on, so I quit dating. I assumed I was frigid."

He said with unexpected gentleness, "When did you find out you weren't?"

"Last night."

That took him by surprise. "Last night? You mean when we were kissing in the honeymoon suite of the Hotel Paraiso?"

She nodded.

"Oh, my God, Diana," Ross proclaimed in husky tones, opening his arms to her.

She took two steps toward him and was immediately engulfed by his embrace. He held her, held her close, held her for dear life. Her whole body was shaking, and her skin was oddly damp.

"Do you have any idea what it does to me to know that I'm the only man you've ever responded to?" he said at last.

"No." Her voice sounded strangely foreign to her own ears. "But I think I can guess."

"I'll bet you can." He laughed as his swelling manhood wedged itself between them. It was a wonderful, masculine laugh. "There is nothing more exciting to a man than the knowledge that he excites a woman."

"The reverse is true, as well," she murmured, savoring her first real taste of feminine power.

Ross gazed down into her eyes. "When I told you I wasn't prepared to make love to you, I meant it literally. I have no way to protect you, Diana. I've been out here in the boonies for a long time. I don't carry little foil packets around with me."

She blushed down to her roots. "I see."

"That was the bad joke last night about being prepared. I wasn't. I'm not."

She took a deep breath and plunged ahead. "In that case, I guess I am."

"Prepared?"

She nodded. "A girlfriend drove me to the airport on Tuesday. She always thought it was a little odd that Yale and I weren't intimate. I never discussed it with her—she just seemed to know somehow. Anyway, she gave me a hug in the car, said something about 'going for it with my fiancé' and stuck a small box in my carryon. I didn't think much about it at the time. I suppose I was a little embarrassed. But it's still there."

Ross didn't even seem to be breathing.

"Do you want me to check?"

"Yes." His voice vibrated with the word.

She went into the sleeping hut, unzipped the side pocket of her carryon and took out a small box. She walked up to him and placed it in his hand. "I guess they even sell them in pretty packages for women now."

"So I hear."

"This is very awkward for me, Ross. I don't know the first thing about the proper etiquette in this situation."

Ross slipped the small box into his pants pocket. Then he looked straight into her eyes. "To hell with the proper etiquette, Diana. Do you want to make love with me?"

"I think so," she said so quietly that she wasn't sure he heard her.

"You need to be certain, sweetheart. Because once we make love, everything will change. There won't be any going back."

She didn't want to go back. She wanted things to change. They had been the same for her for far too long.

She lifted her chin and stated with conviction, "Yes, I want to make love with you, Ross. No strings attached. No risks. No obligations. You've set something free inside me. I want to know what it is."

He took her by the hand and led her into the sleeping hut. "Just one thing. I won't make love while you're wearing another man's engagement ring."

Diana slipped off her diamond, then the gold charm bracelet, as well, and dropped them into his outstretched hand. He picked up his khaki shirt, slipped her jewelry into the pocket and zipped it shut.

Then he knelt before her on the buri palm mat and drew her down to her knees. His arms went around her as he kissed her with a heartrending tenderness.

There was a magical song in the air.

"What's that sound?" she murmured, marveling at its beauty.

"The night bird," stated Ross as he began to unbutton her blouse. "The night bird is serenading us." The material was eased off her shoulders and down her arms, along with her bra. She was nude to the waist. For a moment he only looked at her. Then he said, "You are beautiful," and reached out, cupping the fullness of her ivory breasts in his hands, his thumbs circling their pink-tinged tips.

Diana shivered and touched the flat brown male nipples nestled among the mat of bronzed hair on his chest and watched with fascination as they curled up into two small hard buds. "You're beautiful, too."

Then he bent his head and touched her with the tip of his tongue, flicking it back and forth, from one breast to the other until Diana was quite certain she would go mad. "Ross, please—"

"More?"

She nodded mindlessly. "Please, more."

He drew her deeper into his mouth, nipping on her tender flesh, erotically tugging at her, suckling one swollen peak while his hand fingered the other. Her head fell back, and a low moan issued forth through her parted teeth.

Passion.

Yes, it was passion that he had set free in her last night. It was passion he was unleashing in her even now. It was physical, sexual, intellectual. It was grand and glorious, and it left her feeling intensely alive. Suddenly she wanted to feel Ross all around her, through her, in her. She wanted to know this man as she had known no other. She wanted to do things to him, with him, for him, that she had never even dared to imagine in her wildest dreams.

She caressed his chest and back, pondering the paradox of a man's smooth flesh and hard muscle, marveling at his inherent strength, wondering at his vulnerability. There was no mistaking the hard, pulsing part of him that twitched with each inadvertent brush of her hand, her arm, her thigh.

His hand went to the zipper of her jeans and eased it down halfway, apparently just enough so that he could slip his fingers beneath the waistband of her panties. She could feel his touch on her stomach, then lower to the soft mound of curls between her legs.

"Ross?" She was suddenly uncertain, self-conscious, even a little embarrassed. Her panties were damp. Her body was slick and moist.

"It's all right, Diana," he soothed as he gently fondled her. "I want to feel your sweet response."

There was a tentative probing with the tip of his finger. He dipped into her once, twice, three times, a little farther with each attempt. Then he delved deeper, driving his finger all the way into her, bringing forth a cry from her lips that broke the silence of the night.

Ross covered her mouth with his and swallowed the next passionate outburst as if it were some kind of sweet nectar to drink, as if it endowed him with superhuman strength, as if it simply gave him immense satisfaction to do so.

Instinctively Diana reached for the waistband of his khakis. She eased the zipper down with infinite care once she realized he wore nothing underneath. She trailed her fingers through the patch of hair that encircled his navel and then moved her hand lower.

Ross sucked in his breath. "Diana, sweetheart!"

His ready flesh sprang into her hand. He was smooth and strong and fine and as hard as a rock. She stroked him, caressed him, drew a random pattern from one end to the other, gave the tip a gentle squeeze.

"I'm surprised. I never knew a man's skin could be so soft," she admitted with dreamy amazement.

He laughed a little wildly. "There will be an even bigger surprise in a minute if you keep that up."

She frowned in puzzlement.

He tried to explain. "Let's just say I don't have an overabundance of control right about now."

She still didn't understand. "Why is it a problem?"

"This isn't what I had planned," Ross ground through his teeth in the split second before he lost it altogether and a violent shudder shook his body.

Diana had touched him and he'd gone off like a firecracker on the Fourth of July. It wasn't quite what he'd had in mind, but it had been so damn long, and she was so sweet and yet utterly irresistible....

He would make it up to her. They had all night. It wasn't the end; it was only the beginning.

"You aren't—disgusted, are you?" he asked.

Diana gazed up at him with huge, honest eyes. "Disgusted? Why would I be disgusted? I loved it."

"You loved it?" repeated Ross.

"You were the one who said there's nothing more exciting than knowing you can excite someone else."

"Yes, I did. Didn't I?" he said with a ragged smile. He gave her a bit of a wicked look. "I've also been known to say 'tit for tat.'"

He immediately set out to show her what he meant. Within minutes Diana was writhing beneath him, lifting her hips instinctively, allowing him to divest both of them of the remainder of their clothing.

They were only getting in the way, anyway.

Ross had once asked himself if Diana was cold only on the outside and all hot and sweet on the inside. Was she an ice princess or a woman of passion? He had wanted to know what she would taste like, feel like, be like to make love to. He'd even had a vision of her long, shapely legs wrapped around his body, her beautiful full breasts pressed to him, her nipples rubbing up against his chest, sending chills down his spine, creating goose bumps wherever she touched him.

He had imagined her blond hair, long and loose, all cool and silky, draped across his hot flesh, her lips swollen from his kisses, her body arched toward his as she sought that indescribable release only he could give her.

It was turning out to be a dream come true.

Diana was everything he had imagined, hoped for, dreamed of, even prayed for on several occasions. She was turning out to be the best damn thing that had ever happened to him. It was ironic.

Then he reached for the small box in his pants pocket and took care of the necessities while he still had half a mind to do so.

He brushed his lips along her bare shoulder and felt the involuntary shiver that rippled through her body. He fastened his mouth to hers, slid his hands under her hips and settled her on his lap. He could not bring himself to subject her lovely skin to the hard floor, with or without the buri palm mat.

"Ross—" she mumbled with mild surprise.

"We'll take it slow and easy, sweetheart. There's no need to rush. We have all the time in the world."

He reached between them and found that special spot, that sensitive nub of woman's flesh, that velvet button that gently swelled as he nuzzled it with his fingertip, as he flicked it back and forth until her body began to throb with an even greater need. He slid his finger inside her again. She was hot and wet and ready. He didn't think he could wait another second before burying himself in her. He was in pain, but it was such sweet pain.

"Diana, I need to love you now," he fiercely breathed against her mouth.

"Ross—please, love me! Yes, love me now!" she cried out as if the madness he was creating in her was more than she could bear.

Probing gently at first, then more insistently, then with barely leashed control, he thrust up into her, and little by little, inch by inch, completed the union of their bodies. It was a tight fit.

Diana was panting. "I didn't realize ... I had no idea ... I never once imagined ..."

He was still for a long moment, knowing her body was stretching to accommodate his unaccustomed size.

"Each time it will only get better and better," Ross promised as he began to move, slowly at first and then with increasing frenzy as they were both caught up in a sensual storm of their own creation.

He took them to the edge again and again until they were both mindless with the sensations they created in each other. This was passionate sex at its best: mutual, magical, lovely and moist.

Then Ross felt Diana cling to him, dig her nails into him, as her body convulsed violently around him. She gave one last great shudder and shouted his name, "Ross!"

"Diana!" His hoarse cry of ecstasy rang out only a moment later as he followed her.

Eventually he eased his body from hers, and they stretched out side by side on the bare mats, a shirt half under them, a pair of jeans strewn haphazardly across the floor of the hut, a blouse in a crumpled heap at their feet.

They didn't care.

The night breeze cooled their feverish flesh, dried the sweat from their bodies and left only the wonderful musky essence of their lovemaking.

The roof of the hut was open to the sky above. Diana curled up in his arms and murmured to him, "I can see the stars through the leaves. They seem so close. Like we could almost reach up and touch the heavens."

"Touch the heavens," echoed Ross with a contentment he didn't think he had ever known before.

"Have you ever made love outside?" she asked shyly.

"Honey, it's been so long for me that I can't even remember the last time I made love anywhere."

Her eyes shimmered in the moonlight. "Then it was the first time for both of us."

He liked that idea. "Yup, the first time for both of us." He turned onto his side and ran his hands over her smooth skin. "There has never been another woman like you, Diana."

"There has never been another man like you, Ross."

Her hand slid down the passion-slick skin of his chest to settle momentarily on his waist. Her nails scraped the smooth abdomen, the line of his hip, the sinewy muscle of his thigh in a tantalizing gesture. He heard her take in a deep breath before she daringly moved her hand lower. His body responded instantly.

She seemed pleased with herself. More than that, she seemed thrilled with herself.

She stroked him lovingly. "I never dreamed it could be like this."

"This is no dream," he vowed in a husky tone as it began all over again.

If it was a dream, Ross thought to himself as he covered her mouth with his, then he hoped he would never wake up....

Eleven

————

"What the—?" came a surprised and angry masculine shout. "Bolo! Where in the hell are you? Bolo! Help me!"

It was several minutes before a muffled reply came from some distance away. "I can't."

"What do you mean you can't? Where in the hell are you? On second thought, I don't care where you are. Just get your butt over here and cut me down."

The hired gorilla who went by the nickname of Bolo sounded as if he was yelling from the bottom of a deep well. "I can't help you. I can't even help myself. I'm stuck in some kind of pit."

"Some kind of pit?"

"You know, a hole in the ground."

The first thug suggested sarcastically, "Then climb out."

"There is no way out. This hole's got to be fifteen, maybe even twenty feet deep. The sides are perfectly straight, like sheer rock. I'm stuck."

"So am I," growled the captive aboveground.

Bolo called out to the other strong-arm man, "What happened to you?"

With a disgruntled admission, the answer came back. "I was walking along and my foot got caught in a trap."

"A trap, did you say?"

"Yes, a trap. Now I'm hanging upside down from a tree like some kind of trussed chicken."

"Why not take your semiautomatic and shoot yourself down?" was Bolo's suggestion.

"I would, but my weapon fell out of my hands when I went flying up in the air. Now it's on the ground five feet from me. I can't reach it."

His reply was discouraged, "Crap."

"Yeah. Crap."

"What'll we do?" asked Bolo.

"Wait," answered his companion. "Just wait."

Morning came to the forest. Monkeys began to chatter and swing excitedly from tree to limb to tree limb. Birds took to the wing, calling to each other, warning one another. The jungle had been disturbed by intruders.

The racket awakened Ross and Diana as they lay sleeping high above in the treetops.

Diana pushed herself up on one elbow and rubbed her eyes. "What's all the noise about?"

Ross was stretched out comfortably beside her on the buri palm mats. He reached over, pulled her back into the crook of his arm and said sleepily, "I must have caught a couple of big rats in my rattraps."

"Big rats?" she murmured against his bare shoulder.

"Maybe I snared the goons who were in your room the other night."

Her eyes popped open, and she sat straight up. "You're kidding."

It didn't appear he was going to get any more sleep. "No. I'm not kidding."

"Ross St. Clair, what have you done?"

"Don't worry, honey. I just used a few basically harmless tricks I picked up from the natives on the last island where I lived." He gave a casual shrug. "Plus a technique or two I learned in engineering school."

She looked at him with genuine skepticism. "Are you sure it wasn't in soldier-of-fortune school?"

That made him laugh. He had never thought of MIT being a training ground for soldiers of fortune.

She chewed on her bottom lip and inquired, "Do you think they're hurt?"

"Who?"

"The big rats caught in your traps."

"I doubt it," he said, unconcerned. "I figure they deserve whatever happens to them. Those two goons aren't exactly model citizens, don't forget. They were planning to kidnap you and do God knows what else."

Her mouth thinned for a moment. "I haven't forgotten."

Ross sat up and raised his arms high above his head. "I can't remember the last time I slept so well."

Diana gave him a warm smile. "Me, either."

He dropped a lingering kiss on her mouth. "Pretty amazing, isn't it?"

"Yes, it is," she whispered.

"But a man's work is never done," Ross announced with a melodramatic sigh. "I guess I'd better get dressed and go down to see what I've caught in my rattraps."

Diana moistened her bottom lip. "If it is the two goons from the Hotel Paraiso, does this mean we'll head back to Port Manya today?"

"Yup. That's what it means. But you keep out of sight until I give the all clear. I want to make sure both of the hired gunmen are out of commission before you come down."

"And we wouldn't want to give them any idea of where the hideout is located."

"That's for sure."

She stood up, seemingly unconcerned with her nudity. "I think I'll take a quick shower. Then I'll see what's for breakfast."

Ross watched her lovely lithe form as she moved about the thatched-roof hut. "Probably the same gourmet fare we had for lunch and dinner yesterday," he said with a grimace.

She gave him one those knowing feminine looks. "Silly man. We didn't have any dinner yesterday."

He rubbed his bare belly with his hand. "Maybe that explains why I'm so hungry."

She arched an eyebrow in his direction. "Maybe."

Ross quickly dressed in his standard wrinkled khakis and well-scuffed military boots. He slipped a lethal-looking knife into his belt, grabbed an extra spear and several lengths of sturdy rope.

"What are you going to do?" Diana asked, standing there, clutching Lola's blouse to her bare breasts.

"If I have caught those two thugs, I want to make sure they aren't going anywhere until we get back to Port Manya and inform Sergeant Bok. He'll want to take them into custody."

"And then?"

"And then it's up to the authorities." He threw the ladder over the side. "I'm going to circle around and come in from the opposite direction."

"Another trick you learned in your engineering days," she said, tongue in cheek.

Ross dropped a hard kiss on her mouth. "I'll be back."

Ross nimbly climbed down the hemp ladder and dropped onto the jungle floor.

It was amazing what a little food, a good night's rest and the greatest sex of his life could do for a man's disposition. His feeling of well-being had never been better.

He moved silently through the forest, circling around in a wide arc until he reached the pathway they had followed the day before.

Yup, his traps had been sprung. There they were, Curly and Moe, two of the three stooges he'd seen on the beach that evening as Carlos and his partner had discussed Ms. Diana Winsted and the "merchandise."

Ross casually swung the small razor-sharp machete, blade up, over his shoulder and strolled along the jungle path, whistling under his breath as if he didn't have a care in the world.

"Hey! Hey, mister!" shouted the first gorilla as soon as he spotted Ross.

The man was hanging upside down from a rope, his legs snared by the trap, his face scarlet from anger and all the unaccustomed blood rushing to his head. His shirttails had come loose from his trousers, and his soft, bare belly was sticking out.

It wasn't a pretty sight.

Ross nodded and kept walking.

"Hey, mister, stop! I need your help."

Ross paused, picked up the nasty-looking semiautomatic that had fallen to the jungle floor, twirled it around on his finger, made sure the safety was on and then casually sauntered over to the nearest tree. He leaned back against the trunk, took a toothpick from his shirt pocket, stuck it into the side of his mouth and squinted at the hired hood. "You got a problem?" he inquired laconically.

The brute swore viciously under his breath. "What in the hell does it look like to you?"

Ross took his own good time responding. "Looks to me like you've got a problem."

"I'm not the only one. My buddy is over there in some kind of hole in the ground."

"Booby trap left over from the last world war."

The thug was starting to sweat profusely; it dripped down his face and formed drops of moisture on the tip of his nose. "No kidding," he said.

"No kidding." Ross pushed his khaki hat back off his forehead. "There are booby traps all over this forest. You've got to be real careful where you step."

"I wished I'd known that earlier."

"I'll bet you do," he said in a softly lethal voice.

The thug was starting to panic. "Look, fella, are you going to help me and my buddy, or not?"

"Oh, I'm going to help you all right."

That brought a grin from the trussed chicken. "Great. Then would you mind cutting me down? I've been like this for at least a half hour. I feel like I could puke."

"Sure, I'll cut you down, but first..."

The man's dead-fish eyes—yeah, that's what Simon Ha had called them, dead-fish eyes—narrowed suspiciously. "But first *what?*"

"I have a couple of simple questions to ask you."

At random Ross picked up a sizeable limb that had fallen to the forest floor. He took the razor-sharp machete and whacked the piece of wood in two. His knife was very sharp, and he was obviously very skilled with it.

The man swallowed. "A couple of simple questions?"

Ross went down on his haunches and looked the goon straight in the eye. "Who is Carlos?"

The man was quick. Quicker than Ross anticipated. He played dumb real well. "Carlos? I don't know any Carlos."

"You dead certain?"

"Yeah, I'm certain."

Ross straightened and let the knife fly. The blade whizzed past the thug's head—missing his ear by only inches—and was partially buried in the bark of a tree.

"You're pretty good with that thing," came the half-grudging admiration.

They both knew he was good. Damn good.

Ross preferred to be modest. "I'm not bad. A little out of practice."

"Even if I knew who Carlos was, I couldn't tell you," said the henchman. "I'd be a dead man within a week, anyway."

Ross decided it was time to try a different tact. "Where is the merchandise?"

That brought a mirthless laugh. "What merchandise?"

"I know about the merchandise. I heard Carlos talking on the beach that night."

"Well, goody for you, cowboy. I don't know anything about any merchandise."

Ross's voice hardened to solid rock. "You plug-ugly son of a gun! You were in the lady's hotel room the other night looking for it."

He spit. "You've got no proof."

"Maybe the lady can identify you."

"It was too dark."

"So you admit that you were in her room."

"I admit nothing."

"Maybe you rifled through her belongings in Manila, too, huh?"

The man's features turned rabid. "You're bluffing, cowboy. You haven't got a shred of evidence."

"Maybe not," said Ross as he casually stretched out his long legs. "Maybe I don't need any evidence. On some of these islands there is no law." He gave a well-done laugh. "Hell, on some of these islands there aren't even any people. Maybe I'll take you and your buddy for a ride in my boat. Maybe I'll dump you on a deserted island and let the two of you spend eternity in hell together."

Ross left the first man to think over the prospect of living out his life on a deserted island in the Pacific and sauntered over to the pit. He glanced down at the not-so-tough thug sitting in the bottom of the deep hole. "Have you got anything to say for yourself?"

The trussed chicken bellowed, "Keep your damn mouth shut, Bolo, or I'll shut it for you permanently."

Bolo raised his arm and made an obscene gesture at Ross. "I got nothing to say to you."

"Look, mister, we can't tell you anything. Now, are you going to cut me down or not?"

"I might."

"You might?"

Ross shook his head from side to side. "The thing is, you two made me real mad."

"How'd we do that? We don't even know you."

Ross played mumblety-peg with his machete. "You tried to mess with my woman."

"Your woman? You mean the classy-looking blonde. Hell, we didn't know she was your woman."

He said in a voice as hard as nails, "You know now. If either of you ever go within a continent of her again, I'll cut out your lily-livered hearts and feed them piece by piece to the swamp rats."

The thug hanging from the tree began to nervously look around. "Swamp rats?"

"Nasty things, swamp rats. I saw a swarm of them go crazy once on the frontier in Cotabato." He shuddered. "Never saw a man eaten alive like that before," he said dramatically. "Don't care if I ever do again."

"Hey, mister, you have my solemn word. We won't go anywhere near the woman again. I swear it on my beloved mother's head," vowed the man in the pit.

Ross took care of the thug hanging upside-down first. He wasn't taking any chances with these two snakes, however. He tied the man's hands securely behind his back before he cut him down and marched him to the hole where his partner was imprisoned.

"Jump in."

"What the—?"

"Just do it!"

"But I thought you were going to let us go."

"Then you thought wrong."

"You said you'd cut me down."

"I did cut you down."

With that, Ross sliced through the ropes holding the man's hands, gave him a nudge and watched as he fell into the pit. The man landed on the soft dirt at the bottom, stood up and dusted himself off.

Ross stood and looked down at the pair. "Let me give you two a friendly piece of advice. I think it's time you took up a new occupation. Something a little less hazardous. Something on the other side of the planet."

"If I ever get out of this alive, I'm going back home to my mother," promised the first man.

"It's South America for me," vowed the second.

"It sounds like you two are making some excellent career changes," said Ross.

Then he put his head back and gazed up at the blazing sun. "I'm afraid it's going to be something of a long, hot day for you. But I estimate that Sergeant Bok and his men should be here before nightfall to take you into custody. They'll be more than happy to escort you off the island."

There was grumbling from the pit.

"Adios, gentlemen."

Then Ross circled back to the tree house, covering his tracks as he went. He gave a whistle, and Diana lowered the ladder.

She was dressed in the same ridiculous but endearing outfit that she'd worn the day before, right down to the Tigers baseball cap. Her carryon was packed. The thatched-roof sleeping hut was aired and cleaned out. Food was waiting for him.

"I slaved over a hot stove all morning to prepare your breakfast, sweetheart," she teased, handing him a pack of black-market army rations.

IIc wordlessly wolfed down the food.

"Did you find anything in your rattraps?"

He nodded.

"Were they the two gorillas you suspected?"

"Yup."

"You didn't hurt them, did you?"

Ross laughed. "Of course I didn't hurt them. They're in a nice safe place until Charoon Bok arrives with his deputies." He finished eating. "Are you ready to head back to civilization?"

Diana looked around the sanctuary in the treetops. "I don't suppose we'll ever come back here, will we?"

"I don't suppose we will."

Her eyes were serious. "I'll never forget this place."

"Neither will I," he admitted. "Where the trees meet the sky—that must surely be heaven."

"No," said Diana softly.

Ross frowned. "No?"

Her eyes were golden fire when she whispered, "Heaven is in your arms."

Twelve

"**I** still don't get it," said Ross as they finished searching through her belongings one last time. "We've examined every darn article of clothing you brought with you, every piece of paper, every document, we've even gone through Grimmer's stuff and there is nothing here that qualifies as 'merchandise.'"

"I know. I don't get it, either," said Diana as she flipped her long loose hair back off her shoulders. "Are you sure you didn't misunderstand what the men on the beach said?"

"I'm sure. In fact, I'm positive."

She shrugged. "Then I don't have a clue."

Trying to identify the "merchandise" was just one of many unanswered questions in her life, however. It had been an eventful week. Her otherwise well-ordered existence had literally been turned upside down.

She had flown halfway around the world to meet a fiancé who had mysteriously disappeared "on business" the day before her arrival. A crazy soldier of fortune had met her at the airport and warned her that she was in mortal danger. Puddle jumping to an isolated island in the Celebes Sea, she had met a colorful cast of local characters. Ross had claimed that she was his wife. Thugs had tried to kidnap her. She'd spent a wild and wonderful night of lovemaking in a tree house in the forest, and several more in the honeymoon suite of the Hotel Paraiso.

Now she was back where she'd started, at the Manila Hotel, trying to decide what do do with the rest of her life.

Yes, it had been an eventful week to say the least.

"Maybe we'll never know what they were looking for," she concluded, and stretched out her bare legs along the sofa in the sitting room.

"Maybe not." Ross reached down and began to gently massage her toes and instep. "How are the feet?"

"Between Simon Ha's combat boots and hiking for miles through the jungle, I don't think they will ever be the same," she admitted matter-of-factly.

She would certainly never be the same, but it had nothing to do with her feet.

Nevertheless, she told Ross breezily, "The minute I get back to the States, I'm going to buy myself some comfortable walking shoes. Or maybe a pair of those special sandals they import from Scandinavia that are supposed to be so good for your feet."

"I have never understood why women wear those high-heeled torture devices, anyway," he said, shaking his head.

"Vanity."

"'Vanity, thy name is woman.'"

She corrected him. "Actually the quote is, 'frailty, thy name is woman.'"

"Macbeth?"

Diana shook her head. *"Hamlet."*

Ross looked at her as if his curiosity had been piqued. "I suddenly realize I don't know very much about you."

"No. You don't."

He cleared his throat awkwardly. "I don't have the slightest idea where you went to school. What you studied. Your favorite color. Your favorite flower. Not even what kind of music you like."

"University of Michigan. English literature. Pale blue. Lilacs. Classical and some rock," she answered succinctly. "What about you?"

Ross seemed willing to reciprocate. "MIT. Electrical engineering. Blond." He grinned. "Roses, I guess. Country western and some rock."

"A perfect match," she said with a tight little smile.

Ross looked intently into her eyes. "We are in some ways."

"In some ways," she repeated softly.

"We never did have that talk," he pointed out.

"No, we didn't."

"I guess we've been too busy island-hopping."

"And running away from thugs."

He put his hand on her shoulder with apparent nonchalance. "And making love."

Diana swallowed. "And making love."

There was an unmistakable expression in the agate-colored eyes. "How about staying in tonight?"

"All right," she replied with what she hoped was a casual air.

"Room service?"

"That's fine."

"We'll eat and we'll talk."

"Eat and *talk?*"

"I promise," he said, and she believed him. "Your place or mine?"

Since Ross had taken a room just down the hall from hers, it hardly mattered.

"Mine," said Diana. "But I would like to take a bath and change clothes first."

"I guess a shower and a shave wouldn't hurt me, either," he said, getting to his feet. "A half hour?"

"Make it an hour, and here's a key." She handed it to him. "Let yourself in."

Ross paused at the door of her hotel suite, leaned over and placed a lingering kiss on her mouth. He reluctantly drew away. "I'll be back."

Her voice was husky. "That's what you always say."

"And I always come back."

How long was *always* for a man like Ross St. Clair? That was the question Diana asked herself as she stripped off her clothes and ran a tubful of hot water.

Was there any future with a man who roamed from place to place? Who seemingly went through life without a care in the world? Without a single thought for what tomorrow might bring? Who carried all of his earthly possessions in a single well-worn knapsack?

She slipped into the steamy bathwater and put her head back against the porcelain tub. "He's the wrong kind of man for you, Diana," she said out loud.

But, dear God, he *felt* so right!

She loved the way Ross kissed her, touched her, caressed her, made love to her. She was crazy about the taste of him, the feel of him, the sheer strength of him.

There was more.

She had grown to respect him, to appreciate his wit, his intelligence, his integrity. She believed him to be an honest man, an honorable man, a gentle man.

He was also tough to the core, hard as nails, and quite capable of both violence and vengeance.

He was everything she didn't want in a man, and yet she found him irresistible.

"Damn. Damn. Damn." Diana swore softly as she immersed herself in soap bubbles right up to her chin.

What was she going to do?

Well, to start with, she wasn't going to marry Yale Grimmer. The minute she got back to Grosse Pointe, she would need to begin *undoing* all the plans she had just spent months *doing*. The church and the country club would have to be canceled. Her designer gown returned, or sold, or given away. The wedding invitations junked, maybe even shredded.

"I suppose everyone will think you've gone completely gaga. So be it," she told herself philosophically. There were far worse things than appearing a little foolish.

It would cost a pretty penny to cancel what was to have been the society event of the year. But she could afford it. She could *not* afford to marry the wrong man.

She wasn't sure who Mr. Right was anymore. But she knew for certain that Yale Grimmer was Mr. Dead Wrong.

Diana took a thick cotton washcloth from the towel rack beside the tub, dipped it into the hot bathwater, wrung it out and placed it across her eyes.

She let out a contented sigh.

Sometimes happiness in life got down to the basics. Hot water to bathe in. Clean clothes. Comfortable shoes. Decent food. Air-conditioning. A good firm mattress. Bug spray. Indoor plumbing. Safe drinking water. Just feeling safe, period. These were a few of the things she would never take for granted again, Diana vowed to herself.

She lost track of time. She may even have dozed. At some point she realized that the bathwater had cooled off and the skin on her fingers and toes was beginning to look like wrinkled prunes. She pulled the plug, reached for a towel and stepped out of the tub.

She slipped into her favorite wrapper, padded barefoot into the adjoining bedroom, sat down at the dressing table and began to run a comb through her damp hair. It brought back a rush of memories. That first night in the honeymoon suite at the Hotel Paraiso. The tree house in the forest. Showering under a rain barrel. Making love with Ross—his hands, his face, his lips buried in her wet hair.

"Oh . . ." she groaned aloud.

Diana stared at herself in the mirror. She had no regrets. She'd do it all over again if given the chance. But as hard as she tried, she could not imagine a future with Ross St. Clair.

A bleak expression looked back at her. Could she imagine a future *without* him?

Her voice lacked its customary sparkle as she muttered out loud, "You're in trouble now. Big trouble. What are you going to do about it?"

"Funny you should say that, my dear. I was just thinking the very same thing," came a familiar male voice from behind her.

Diana turned. She sucked in her breath. Then exclaimed in a half surprised, half angry tone, "Yale!"

Thirteen

Yale looked exactly the same. Tall. Good-looking. Brown hair. Brown eyes. Slender build. He'd been the quarterback on his college football team.

Diana wasn't sure why she'd expected him to have changed. Then she realized it was because *she* had changed.

She pushed back the chair in front of the mirrored vanity, rose to her feet and secured the tie of her wrapper more tightly around her waist. Her fiancé stood in the doorway of the bedroom and waited for her to come to him.

She walked across the room, paused for a moment in front of him, reached up, placed a lukewarm kiss of greeting on his cheek and said, "Hello, Yale." Then she brushed past him and went into the sitting room, knowing that he would follow.

It was improper for a gentleman to be in a lady's boudoir, even if they were engaged to be married. Appearances must be maintained, after all. Proprieties must be observed.

Yale Grimmer had always been a stickler for appearances and proprieties.

His mouth thinned with a hint of disapproval. "I'll wait while you get dressed."

Diana glanced down at the modest bathrobe that covered her from neck to ankle. "I'm decent."

His brown brows, the same color as his hair, drew together. "Where have you been?"

"Taking a bath," she replied innocently.

"I don't mean in the past five minutes." His eyes narrowed. "Where in the hell have you been for the past five days?"

"Where in the hell have you been?" Diana countered with uncharacteristic bluntness.

For a moment Yale seemed taken aback by her outburst, but recovered admirably. His voice was laced with reproach as he informed her, "*I* have been running my tail off taking care of business. *I* have been trying to secure a future for the two of us. *I* have responsibilities, you know. I am in charge of the entire operation for the company in Asia and the Pacific."

She bit her tongue. "Yes, I know. I'm well aware of your corporate responsibilities." He had told her often enough.

Diana took a long, hard look at the man she had almost married. Yale wasn't safe; he was a bore. He was handsome, yes, but bland. There was no character in his face, no strength, no passion.

He was dressed in conservative business attire for this part of the world: dark brown slacks, dark brown shoes, white shirt. There was nary a wrinkle to him, despite the heat and humidity. Every strand of his salon-styled hair was in place. He was completely clean shaven. His eyebrows were barber trimmed. His complexion had the slightest touch of a tan, just enough to make him appear the clean-cut, all-American boy.

All-American *man,* she corrected herself.

That was the moment it became crystal clear to Diana. The real difference between Yale Grimmer and Ross St. Clair was the difference between a boy and a man.

Odd, but Yale seemed years younger, although both men were in their mid-thirties.

Something else suddenly dawned on her. "By the way, how did you get into my hotel room?"

Yale dug into his pocket and produced a standard key. "I used a key. The suite is officially registered to the corporation. I did knock. In fact, several times. Apparently you didn't hear me."

He was lying.

She didn't know why, but she was positive there had been no knock on her door.

"I think I'll have a drink before dinner," he said, stepping behind the bar. "May I fix you one, my dear?"

"No. Thank you, anyway." Somehow Diana knew she'd need a clear head in the next few minutes. Something was going on here. She didn't know what it was. But she had a feeling she was going to find out.

Yale poured himself a shot of Chivas Regal, added a splash of soda to the glass and sauntered over to the plush sofa as if he owned the world, the hotel suite and Diana. In that order. Then he demanded in a deceptively mild tone, "So, where have you been?"

"You wouldn't believe me if I told you," she muttered with a touch of sarcasm.

"When did you pick up this annoying habit of mumbling under your breath? It's not like you," he observed.

"Maybe I've changed."

"I can't imagine why. You were perfect the way you were," he said.

"The perfect debutante. The perfect hostess. The perfect future corporate wife."

"Yes. As I said, you were perfect."

"And as a woman?"

He frowned at her. It was obvious Yale Grimmer didn't have a clue what she was talking about.

"We haven't seen each other in nearly three months. That's a long time," Diana proposed, tossing her hair back over one shoulder.

"You always used to wear your hair swept up. I prefer it up," Yale commented as he sipped his Scotch.

"I wear it down most of the time now," she said pointedly.

He seemed to put the subject of her hairstyle from his mind and said with ill-concealed impatience, "You were about to tell me where you've been."

"Well, for one thing," she replied, her chin held high, "I was on the island of Port Manya because you telephoned and asked me to join you there."

A tinge of color crept up Yale's neck and onto his cheeks. "You were on Port Manya?"

"Yes," she flared. "At the hotel where you were supposed to meet me."

The answer stupefied him. "But there was no Diana Winsted registered at the Hotel Paraiso when I inquired."

Ooops!

She deftly sidestepped the subject. "Well, when I inquired, there *was* a Yale Grimmer registered, but no one had seen him since the day before when he went off to talk to a fisherman about renting a boat."

His voice held no apology. "I had some unexpected business come up. But I returned within forty-eight hours, and you weren't there. It was dashed inconvenient, I'll tell you," he added in a sulky tone.

Diana had had just about enough. Indeed, she'd had more than enough. "Well, it wasn't exactly convenient for me to fly all the way to some godforsaken island for nothing, either." It was time to take the bull by the horns. "Tell me something, Yale."

He glanced at her over the rim of his glass. "Yes?"

"Who is Carlos?"

Yale choked on his drink; the amber-colored Scotch dripped onto his otherwise pristine white shirt. "Carlos? I don't know anyone named Carlos."

He was a bad liar.

Diana tried a different tact. "What is the 'merchandise'?"

This time he wasn't quick enough to hide his astonishment. His face flushed scarlet. "What the—?" He slammed the glass down on the coffee table and sprang to his feet. "How did you find out about that?"

She regarded him with an air of cool superiority. "It's a long story."

"We've got time."

Not as much as he thought. She took a deep breath and said, "It all started when Ross—"

Yale immediately interrupted her and rudely demanded, "Who in the hell is Ross?"

His words acted like a trigger release. The man was going to get the full treatment. It was no more than he deserved.

Diana traced an imaginary line along the edge of the mahogany bar with her fingertip and said blithely, "Ross is this soldier of fortune who tried to pick me up at the airport the day I arrived in Manila."

Yale Grimmer was visibly stunned. "My God, Diana, what's happened to you?"

"More than you'll ever know, or could ever imagine," she said, facing him squarely. "Why don't you sit down again, Yale. You seem slightly shell-shocked."

"If you don't mind, I prefer to stand," he snapped at her peevishly.

Diana shrugged her shoulders and continued with her story. "It all began at the airport. There was this man—"

"This soldier of fortune?" he interjected.

She nodded. "This soldier of fortune was waiting for me. Initially I thought Ross had been sent by you, or by the company. He was holding up a sign with my name written on it."

Her one-time fiancé made an inarticulate noise and stared down into his half-empty glass.

"As it turned out, of course, he was a complete stranger. He'd raced to the airport to warn me that I was in trouble. Big trouble, he claimed."

This was a little too much for Yale Grimmer. "I think I will sit down."

Diana was almost enjoying herself now. "I didn't believe him at first. And when he wouldn't let go of my arm, I threatened to scream bloody murder."

"My God, you were openly accosted in broad daylight in a public airport?"

"It wasn't really as bad as it sounds," she said, the golden brown eyes flickering almost humorously. "Anyway, I didn't believe one word of the crazy story he tried to tell me."

"I should hope not."

"Until later."

That brought his head up. "Until later?"

"When I went upstairs and discovered that my hotel suite had been ransacked."

The sideways glance he gave her was disconcertingly shrewd. "Did you notify hotel security, or the police?"

She gave her head a shake. "Ross didn't recommend it. The red tape and all. We decided to check ourselves to see if anything had been stolen."

"Had it?"

"No." She made a sudden and vigorous gesture with both her hands. "That was the strangest part of all. Not a single thing was missing."

"That is strange."

"A few minutes after that, you called."

His eyes touched hers briefly. "God, Diana, why didn't you warn me?"

"You mean, *tell* you?"

"Yes, why didn't you tell me what was going on?"

"Our connection wasn't very good. I was having trouble hearing you," she said by way of an explanation. "Besides, there wasn't anything you could do. You were hundreds of miles away on Port Manya."

His shoulders drooped. "You fool. You bloody stupid little fool," he growled.

For a minute Diana thought she'd heard him incorrectly. "I beg your pardon?"

"Nothing," he said, his expression grim.

"The next morning I went to the airport as you'd instructed and caught the nine-thirty flight to Port Manya," she said matter-of-factly. "Ross came along."

Yale's handsome face tightened. "You invited another man to come with you?"

"Of course not," she said tersely. "I didn't realize what his plans were until I got on the plane, and there he was."

"I'm beginning to dislike this soldier of fortune of yours already."

If he only knew the half of it!

Diana took a deep breath and plunged ahead. "Anyway, when we arrived on the island and you were nowhere to be found, Ross thought it would be wise for us to pretend we were married."

That brought Yale right up out of his seat. "The damn fool did *what?*"

She leapt to Ross's defense. "He isn't, he wasn't, a damn fool. At the time it seemed like a good idea. It was to protect me. The culture on Port Manya is very conservative. A single woman traveling on her own, without a chaperon, is regarded with great—suspicion."

"The guy sounds like a world-class con artist to me." Yale looked at her as though she had taken leave of every one of her senses. "Don't tell me that you ended up sharing a hotel room with him."

Diana straightened her shoulders and said with as much dignity as she could muster, which was a considerable amount, "Yes, I did."

He reached out for her hand and gripped her fingers so tightly she winced. "You weren't the American couple staying in the honeymoon suite?"

Refusing to cringe in the face of Yale Grimmer's disapproval, Diana confirmed, "As a matter of fact, we were."

"Did you sleep with him?"

"It's a strange thing about men," she said, ignoring his implication.

"What is?"

"Sex."

His voice rose, rich with anger. "Sex?"

She nodded. "That was one of the first questions Ross asked about you."

The once-handsome face was scarlet with outrage. "The guy had the nerve to ask if you were sleeping with me?"

She could think of nothing more appropriate to say than a simple, "Yes."

"Did you tell him?" asked Yale coloring angrily.

She managed to withdraw her fingers from his grasp. "Not at the time."

"I should hope not."

"But he seemed to know, anyway. I guess it's a sixth sense, an instinct—some men have it and some men don't."

"And he has it," said Yale gloomily.

She flashed him a broad smile. "In spades."

Yale staunchly declared, "I have always held you in the highest regard, Diana. I respected you. I adored you. I put you up on a pedestal."

She deflated his hot air-filled balloon with a single word. "Bull."

Suddenly Diana realized that she didn't like Yale Grimmer very much. The man was vain. Self-centered. Chauvinistic. Shallow. A bad liar. And insincere.

"You are not the woman I thought you were," he said icily. "You've changed."

"Yes, I have. Thank God."

"Did you sleep with your soldier of fortune?" he asked venomously.

"Yes."

"Of your own free will?"

"Absolutely."

"Son of a—" His features hardened. "You fell for the bastard, didn't you?"

She was incensed. "Ross is not a bastard. He happens to be an out-of-work engineer."

"You've fallen in love with a drifter. A man who doesn't even have a job. A man who couldn't afford to pay your clothes bill for one month. Have you lost your mind?''

"Possibly."

"You're making a big mistake."

"I don't think so. Marrying you, now that would have been a big mistake."

"The wedding is off."

"I certainly hope so."

"Dammit, Diana, how could you do this to me?"

"It has nothing to do with you, Yale," she declared archly. "It was just one of those things."

He shook his head, and a bitter laugh escaped. "If only I had been there when your plane landed."

"But you weren't. And there is no going back now," she said firmly. "Naturally I will return the diamond engagement ring you gave me."

Yale looked at her hand for the first time since entering the hotel suite. "Where is your engagement ring?"

Diana glanced down at her ringless finger. "Now, let me see . . . when did I take it off?"

"Cripes, you don't even remember!"

She pursed her lips in thought. Then it all came back to her. It was just before Ross had made love to her in the forest tree house. He had stashed both her engagement ring and her charm bracelet in his shirt. She hadn't given either one a thought since. She assumed both pieces of jewelry were still in his pocket.

Yale's lips went white. "Where is the gold charm bracelet I gave you?"

Diana found herself in the grip of an odd feeling of danger. "I don't know. Why?"

He stated unequivocally, "I want the bracelet returned, as well."

"But it was a birthday present."

"I don't care. I don't want you to have it now. Not after what you've done."

She didn't believe him. Not entirely. Yale wanted the bracelet back all right. But he was lying about the reason.

She sighed and gave a nonchalant shrug. "I don't have the charm bracelet anymore."

Yale was next to her in a shot. "You don't have it anymore?"

"No."

"You little fool," he said, quite fearless with resentment. "It was the bracelet all along."

Her gaze narrowed. "What do you mean 'it was the bracelet all along'?"

He was nearly shouting at her now. "The merchandise. The bloody merchandise. It was on the bracelet, you stupid bitch."

Yale Grimmer was suddenly in a rage. It was an ugly sight. This was not the man she'd thought she had known, Diana realized. "What was on the bracelet?" she asked, managing to keep her wits about her even though he was falling apart.

He swore viciously, using words she had never heard from him before. "A quarter of a million dollars."

Her eyes grew round as saucers. "What?"

"One of the charms on the bracelet was a coin."

She nodded and agreed. "Yes." It had never been her personal favorite, however.

"That coin was one of a kind. To the right collector it was worth at least a quarter of a million dollars. Maybe more."

She had an awful, sinking feeling in the pit of her stomach. "Yale, what have you done?"

He grabbed her by the arms and gave her a shake. "If I don't get that bracelet back, Diana, I'm a dead man."

A voice as hard as nails came from the doorway behind them. "You're a dead man, Grimmer, if you don't take your hands off my woman."

Fourteen

—

"*Your* woman?"

"My woman." Ross liked the sound of it; he nearly said it again.

Yale Grimmer dropped his hands, quickly stepped away from Diana, shook his head and, with an incredulous expression, looked from Ross back to her. "The guy is a Neanderthal. Where did you get him?"

"I told you," she said with a perfectly straight face, "at the airport."

Ross St. Clair nearly lost it at that point and laughed out loud. He had heard most of the conversation between Diana and her ex-fiancé from the doorway. She had held her own very nicely. Very nicely, indeed. But there were still a few unanswered questions, a few loose ends to tie up.

He took a menacing step toward the other man. "At least I know how to take care of my own, Grimmer. You don't deserve a woman like Diana."

The brown-haired businessman hooted. "And you do?"

Ross advanced another step. "I wouldn't hide behind a woman's skirts. I wouldn't use her as a courier. I wouldn't put her life in jeopardy for a lousy quarter of a million bucks."

Diana echoed. "Put my life in jeopardy?"

"Her life was never in any danger," claimed Yale, nervously licking his lips.

"You lily-livered, chickenhearted piece of—" Ross paused and smiled apologetically at Diana. "Since there is a lady present, I won't tell you what I really think of you, Grimmer. I should beat you to within an inch of your life for what you did. I was there. I heard every word. So don't lie to me," he spit out as he moved closer.

Yale backed up. "What do you mean *you* were there?"

Two chips of hard, agate-colored stone bored right through the coward. "I was on the beach that night. I heard the conversation between you and Carlos. I know he made threats against Diana." Then Ross perfectly mimicked the man's husky, cigar-smoking tone of voice, "'We expect the merchandise to be in our hands by the end of the week, or Ms. Winsted will pay the price with her lovely head.'"

Yale Grimmer paled. "My God, you were there!"

"Yup."

"We didn't know anyone was listening."

"I assumed you didn't." Ross added nonchalantly, "I suppose the goons with the semiautomatic weapons were hired to insure that there weren't any eavesdroppers."

"Then how—" Grimmer was obviously having difficulty taking it all in. "Then how did you manage it?"

Diana piped up. "He's a soldier of fortune."

Her former fiancé turned to her for an instant. "I thought you said he was an out-of-work engineer."

She looked down her nose at him and said informatively, "The average American will change his/her profession at least three times during his/her lifetime."

"Who knows what I'll be next?" added Ross dryly.

"You can be anything you want to be," said Diana, as if she had all the confidence in the world in him.

"Thank you, sweetheart."

"Good grief," muttered Yale.

Ross turned his attention to the louse standing in front of him and said, "I believe the lady asked you a question or two that you haven't bothered to answer, mister."

Yale attempted to bluff his way out of it. "I don't remember any questions."

"Then let me refresh your memory. To begin with, who is Carlos?"

Grimmer's voice sank almost to a whisper. "I don't know anyone named Carlos."

Ross laughed, shook his head as though he were genuinely bewildered and said in a tone that somehow managed to be both soft and lethal at the same time, "You know, that's the same doggone answer I got from those two thugs I trapped in the jungle." In an aside to Diana, he admitted, "Although I do think Bolo would have talked . . . in the end."

The man in front of him swallowed and said faint-heartedly, " In the end?"

Ross frowned and concluded, after due considera-tion, "It was probably the swamp rats."

Yale Grimmer appeared appalled. "Swamp rats."

Ross reconsidered. "Maybe it was my machete."

"Your *what?*"

"I don't like to brag, Grimmer, but I'm pretty handy with a machete. Maybe I could show you sometime, too."

Diana's eyes narrowed in reprimand. "You didn't hurt those men you caught in the jungle, did you, Ross?"

He was wounded. "I promised I wouldn't, dar-ling."

She patted his muscular arm. "I know. But some-times when you get mad you forget."

"I didn't forget this time. I said I wouldn't hurt them and I didn't." There was a slightly feral expres-sion on his face as he tacked on, "Much."

Yale forced himself to ask, yet it was obvious he didn't want to. "What did those two thugs do?"

Ross grunted. "They tried to mess with my woman."

Diana clarified. "They tried to kidnap me from the Hotel Paraiso. I think they were looking for your merchandise." She added as an afterthought, "I do hope Sergeant Bok found them in time."

Suddenly Yale Grimmer looked as if he needed a strong drink. Perhaps several. "Who is Sergeant Bok?"

Ross retaliated. "Who is Carlos?"

"I can't tell you."

"Then I can't tell you who Sergeant Bok is."

He tried appealing to Diana. "For God's sake, help me!"

Ross watched her with a great deal of satisfaction as she said, "I'm sorry, Yale. I can't."

"But after all we've been to each other."

"We were nothing to each other," she corrected. "In fact, we were less than nothing. We didn't know the first thing about one another. We weren't in love. We weren't in lust. We weren't even friends."

"We were," he pleaded.

She looked at Yale as if she had never seen him before in her life. "A very wise and wonderful man once said that if I stayed in this part of the world I would find the veneer of civilization peeled away. He told me that sooner or later each of us is exposed for exactly who and what we are." Her eyes narrowed. "You are a king-size rat, Yale. You've made your bed, now you'll just have to sleep in it."

"But I'm in trouble. Big trouble," he whined.

Ross didn't say a word. He hoped Diana wouldn't, either. Let Grimmer hang himself without their help.

There was only silence until the desperate man began talking again. He paced back and forth in front of the coffee table. "All right, I admit it. I do know somebody named Carlos. He's a big-time dealer."

"A dealer in what?"

"Imports/exports."

Ross waited. "That usually means smuggling."

"Usually," admitted Grimmer. "Anyway, Carlos and I made a deal. He would find a buyer. I would supply the merchandise."

"And?" he prompted.

"Carlos paid me twenty-five thousand in advance as a show of good faith. The rest of the money was due on delivery."

Ross was genuinely curious. "Where did the deal go sour?"

Yale ran his hand through his usually immaculate hair; the result was a frazzled appearance. "Apparently word got out to certain other interested parties that a rare, one-of-a-kind coin was going to be sold." He glanced up at the taller man. "There are collectors who will stop at nothing to own something of which there is only one."

Ross was entirely unsympathetic. "I'll just bet they are."

Grimmer went on. "I got another offer. Two offers, actually. That was the reason I was on Port Manya. That's why I needed to rent a boat from a local fisherman. Some of my clients prefer to meet anonymously and in very private places."

"Like out at sea."

The suddenly loquacious wheeler-dealer nodded. "Out at sea. Deserted beaches. In the dead of the night."

"Did you know that Carlos sent his goons to search Diana's hotel suite her first night here?"

"I swear to God, I didn't. Not until she told me a few minutes ago."

"That is very fortunate for you." Both men seemed to understand how narrow Grimmer's escape from a well-earned punch in the nose had been. "Did you realize his hired henchmen followed you to Port Manya?"

Yale was sweating bullets. "No. I guess Carlos found out somehow."

"Found out what?" inquired Ross, refusing to let his fish squirm off the hook.

Grimmer glanced away for a moment. "The other interested parties had also given me a down payment on the coin."

"In other words, they each gave you up-front money."

"Yes." Yale seemed to think he had been very clever. "One collector of rare *objets d'art* from Singapore handed over fifty thousand in cash." His eyes glittered. "Imagine fifty thousand American dollars in small unmarked bills. There was no way to trace it. No taxes to pay. It was pure profit."

Ross leaned back against the mahogany bar and folded his arms across his chest. "In other words, you intended to fleece them all but good."

He blew out his breath. "That was the idea."

"Dear Lord, Yale!" Diana's hand flew to her mouth. "How did you expect to get away with a hare-brained scheme like that?"

His eyes were still glittering. "I had several very clever forgeries made. You had the original coin, of course, Diana. I figured I'd keep the down payments, sell the genuine article to the highest bidder and disappear before anyone was the wiser."

"You're not even an honest crook," she scolded.

"You're also a damn stupid one. You'll be lucky not to get yourself killed," Ross observed coolly.

Desperate, he looked from one to the other. "That's why I have to get the bracelet back."

Ross immediately stepped forward and informed him, "Diana wasn't lying to you. She doesn't have the bracelet and she doesn't know where it is. The last time either of us laid eyes on it was in the jungle."

Yale sank down onto the nearest chair and buried his head in his hands. "Then I'm a dead man."

"Not necessarily," he said after a moment. "There might be another way."

"I can't imagine what it is," Yale admitted, lifting his head. He had aged ten years in ten minutes.

Ross measured out controlled calmness. "You could try being honest for a change. You could give the money back."

A burst of dark laughter escaped the man sitting down. "I've already spent most of it. And even if I hadn't, you don't know what these people are like. They'll kill you for just *trying* to double-cross them."

"Then I guess you should have thought of that before you double-crossed them."

Brown eyes went blank. "There's no hope for me. I may as well throw myself off the top of the tallest building in Manila."

"I'm tempted to let you," said Ross. "But it might upset Diana. I don't like having Diana upset. So I'll tell you what we're going to do."

Yale glanced up. He stared at him for a half a minute and then demanded to know, "Just who the hell are you?"

The woman beside him jumped in first. "He is a gentleman in the truest sense of the word."

"Just a man like any other man," said Ross. He meant it for her, not Grimmer.

"A man like no other man," whispered Diana, gazing up at him with what looked like love shining in her eyes.

Ross wanted this business settled and done with. He had more important things to see to: like Diana, like his own future.

He said, "I'll write down a few words on your behalf to Sergeant Charoon Bok. He's a good man. He's been investigating illegal smuggling in the otherwise peaceful waters around his island. Take the morning flight to Port Manya and find Sergeant Bok immediately. Maybe he'll make a deal with you."

"A deal?"

"Information in exchange for your safety. It's done all the time."

Yale Grimmer eyed him with suspicion. "Why are you doing this for me?"

"I'm not doing it for you. I'm doing it for Diana. She's a warm, loving, tenderhearted, concerned woman. Sometimes to a fault. Frankly I don't want your life, or death, weighing on her conscience."

Diana took the opportunity to thread her fingers through his. She gave his hand an appreciative squeeze. "Darling, do you have my engagement ring?"

"Ooops, I nearly forgot." Ross dug into his pocket and took out the diamond. He gazed down into her eyes. "What do you want me to do with it?"

"Give it to him."

"Are you certain?"

"One hundred percent."

"You could trade it in on a whole lot of fancy baubles. Or a few hundred pairs of combat boots."

They both laughed, and it was obvious that Yale Grimmer had no idea why they thought it was so funny.

"I don't need fancy baubles. I have a good sturdy pair of combat boots. Besides, I believe it is customary for the woman to return the ring when she officially breaks off her engagement to a man."

"Whatever you say." Ross unceremoniously tossed the ring into Grimmer's lap. He just managed to catch it.

Diana added, "Besides, I think you're going to need a good lawyer, Yale. And they don't come cheap."

"What I really need is that damn bracelet," he muttered, without so much as a thank-you for the ring.

Ross had had enough. In fact, he'd had more than enough to last him a lifetime. He picked Yale Grimmer up out of the chair, grasped him firmly by the elbow and escorted him to the door of the hotel suite. "What you really need is to get out of here before I change my mind about beating you to within an inch of your life.''

Yale turned white as a ghost.

"Say goodbye, Diana."

"Goodbye, Yale," she dutifully called out to her ex-fiancé.

Sticking out his hand, palm up, Ross demanded of the other man, "Give me the key you have to this room. You won't be needing it anymore. I'll return it to the hotel for you."

Grimmer silently handed him the key.

Ross called over his shoulder, "Just walking Yale to the elevator, sweetheart. I'll be back in a minute and we'll order dinner."

"Hurry back."

On the way to the elevator, Yale Grimmer tried to get in one more dig. "Diana's expensive. Like I said, you won't be able to afford to pay her clothes bill for even one month."

Sometimes a man had to use whatever weapons were at his disposal. Ross figured this was one of those times.

As he hurried the small-time crook along the corridor, he ground through his teeth, "I don't believe it will be as much of a problem as you seem to think."

Yale snorted. "Do you have any idea how much Diana Winsted pays for a pair of shoes alone?"

"I have a pretty good idea."

"How could you possibly manage to keep her in the style she has always been accustomed to?"

"I'll manage."

That brought a nasty retort. "Where would you get money like that?"

Ross arched one well-done brow. "Have you ever heard of the St. Clairs of Phoenix and Palm Springs?"

"Hell, yes, who hasn't? They must own half of Arizona."

"The son owns a healthy chunk of California and Hawaii, too, as a matter of fact."

Grimmer was green with envy. "The bastard must be rolling in it."

"He is." The elevator gave a soft ping, the doors slid open and Ross shoved Grimmer inside. He reached around the corner and pressed his finger on the button for a moment. "I don't believe Diana has ever mentioned my full name."

"I don't believe she has."

There was a moment of anticipation. "It's Ross Matthew St. Clair."

"You're *that* St. Clair?"

He grinned. "Guilty as charged. I just wanted you to rest easy knowing I can keep Diana in clothes."

As the elevator doors closed, Yale Grimmer was standing there, eyes wide, mouth half-open, muttering to himself, "Son of a bitch."

Fifteen

"**D**id Yale get on his way all right?" inquired Diana, glancing up from the room service menu she was studying.

Ross closed the door of the hotel suite behind him and said, "As far as I know. I walked the man to the elevator. Even pushed 'L' for lobby for him."

"I don't know what I ever saw in Yale Grimmer," she admitted with a sigh. "I thought he was such an outstanding, upright and honest member of the human race. Here he turns out to be a world-class rat and a world-class liar."

"I suppose we all stretch the truth now and then," reasoned Ross as he roamed around the sitting room. "And there is always lying by omission."

Diana wasn't sure what he was getting at, but she refused to face it on an empty stomach. "What are you in the mood for?'' she said, perusing the selections for dinner.

"I'm in the mood for love," he sang softly and slightly off-key. It was very endearing.

Her arched brows rose high. "You promised we were going to stay in tonight to *eat* and to *talk,* in that order."

His expression was one of mild sheepishness. "I did, didn't I?"

"Yes, you did."

He showed his white teeth in a sardonic smile. "I wonder whatever possessed me to make such a foolish promise."

Diana held up her forefinger. "One, because we're both hungry." She raised a second finger. "Two, because we need to have a serious talk."

"You're right on both counts, of course," acknowledged Ross. "Why don't you go ahead and order dinner? Surprise me."

"All right."

He made himself comfortable in a corner of the sofa. "And include a bottle of champagne."

"Are we celebrating?"

"I certainly hope we will be," came in a determined voice.

Dinner had been eaten and enjoyed, the dirty dishes cleared away by a polite, uniformed waiter. A bottle of champagne was chilling in a silver bucket at one end of the sofa. There were two crystal glasses filled and sitting on a tray on the coffee table. The lamps were turned low. There was music softly playing somewhere in the background, and the lights of the city were visible through the large picture window in front of them.

It was the perfect romantic setting.

So why were she and Ross suddenly feeling so awkward and uncomfortable with each other?

Diana decided to break the ice. "Who wants to go first?"

Ross stretched his arm out along the back of the cushions and placed a hand lightly on her shoulder. "Why don't we take turns?"

"Every other one?"

"Something like that." There was a moment of silence. "You can start."

She was willing. "All right. Why did you lie to Yale about the gold charm bracelet?"

Ross frowned. "I didn't think he deserved to get it back after what he did to you."

"You were very upset about him using me as a courier, weren't you?" she inquired carefully.

There was an uncompromising hardness about both his features and his manner as Ross confessed to her, "I don't think anything has ever made me angrier."

"Not in your entire life?"

"Not in my entire life. I would loathe any man who would use a woman, any man who would put a woman's life in jeopardy. The fact that Grimmer did it to you only made it ten times worse. A thousand times worse." He took a deep breath and expelled it. "When I was a teenager, maybe even a little younger, my parents drummed one thing into me."

"What was that?"

"'Let your conscience be your guide, Ross. Especially when it comes to girls and women.'"

Her throat was suddenly full. "And you've never forgotten what they said."

"And I have never forgotten."

"I think I'd like your parents."

"I think they'd be crazy about you," he murmured.

"Now it's your turn," Diana reminded him.

"Hold out your hand," instructed Ross.

She did as she was told.

He dug into his shirt pocket, brought out the gold charm bracelet and dropped it into her palm.

She fingered the charms until she came to the coin. "It was never my favorite, but a quarter of a million dollars..."

"It's a lot of money."

"Yes, I suppose it is."

"What are you going to do with it?"

She frowned. "Do with it?"

"The bracelet, and the coin, belong to you."

But the bracelet, its monetary worth and the man who had given it to her as a birthday present were no longer of any value to her. She would never wear it again.

Diana held the bracelet out toward Ross. "I don't want it. I liked it better when it was just another charm bracelet. You take it."

"Me?"

She placed the jewelry in his hands and closed his fingers around the cold metal. "I want you to have it."

"Why?" he asked softly.

She hesitated, then came right out and told him. "I think you are a unique human being, Ross St. Clair. I meant every word when I said you can be anything you want to be." Tears welled in the back of her eyes. "I know you don't have a lot of money. Maybe you can sell the coin and start all over again, create a whole new life for yourself."

He smiled at her. "I already intend to do that. But I don't want the coin, Diana."

"You don't?"

"No, sweetheart, I don't. But I have an idea what we can do with it."

He had her rapt attention now.

"What?"

She watched as he got a faraway look in his eyes. Oh, those eyes that were neither green, nor brown, nor blue, but a rare and wonderful combination of all three!

His voice was deep and rich; it wove a spell around her. "I know of a small, isolated island in the Celebes Sea. The people are poor, but hardworking. There is no school. Just a dusty main street with a few ramshackle buildings and a funny run-down hotel."

"Hotel Paraiso. Hotel Paradise."

Ross continued, "We could sell the coin and give the money to Port Manya. They could build their schoolhouse and afford to hire a teacher."

"Pablo could learn to read."

"And all the other island children, too."

It was an inspired idea. "Yes," breathed Diana. "It's the least we can do under the circumstances."

"Under the circumstances?"

She suddenly lost her nerve. What if she were mistaken? What if Ross didn't feel the same way about her as she felt about him? What if she had misread his intentions? What if their passion for each other began and ended with pure physical attraction?

Dear God, what if he didn't love her?

There were worse things than looking a fool. There were worse things than being rejected. There were worse things than telling a man you loved him and finding out he didn't love you in return.

What was worse?

Playing it safe. Being afraid. Keeping your mouth shut, sometimes. Never knowing passion. Never kissing Ross again. Allowing him to walk out of her life without telling him how much she adored him, wanted him, desired him, loved him.

Diana took a deep breath, steeled herself for whatever lay ahead, turned to Ross and declared in an impassioned voice, "It's the least I can do under the circumstances because it was on Port Manya that I fell in love."

He seemed to stop breathing. "Fell in love?" It was as if he wasn't sure he'd heard her correctly.

It was all there in her eyes if he cared to look. "It was on Port Manya that I fell in love with you."

Ross framed her face with his hands. "Are you sure?"

"Yes. I've never been more sure of anything in my life."

"How? How in the hell do you know?" His voice didn't sound quite like him.

She reached up and, with a feather-light caress, touched his brow, his cheek, his lips, his jaw, with her fingertips. "It was very simple, really. I tried to imagine my life without you. I couldn't."

Something seemed to break loose inside Ross. He brought her face firmly up to his and muttered against her mouth, "I love you so much I don't even care if we're right or wrong for each other. I don't give a damn if we're good or if we're bad together. I can't live my life another minute if I don't know for certain you'll be in it."

"I will be. I promise," she vowed, her voice shaking with emotion.

He drew her into his arms, pulled her across the sofa and onto his lap, held her so close it was as if he never intended to let her go. "Say it again. Please, say it again, Diana. I want the words. I need the words. I've waited for so bloody long to hear them."

She gazed into his eyes, his beautiful eyes, and said, her voice breaking, "I love you, Ross. I'll always love you."

He held her to him fiercely. "I love you, Diana. I love you with all my heart and my soul and my body," he pledged.

"I will love you for richer or poorer, in sickness and in health, for as long as we live," she murmured, reciting part of the traditional wedding vows.

He held her gaze. "You honestly don't care if I'm poor?"

"I honestly don't care. It doesn't matter to me. Only you matter. Only you, Ross."

Diana could feel him watching her. "Then you wouldn't care if I were rich?"

"No—" she laughed "—but you aren't."

His expression was deadly serious. "But I am."

"You are what, darling?" she murmured, far more interested in kissing him than in continuing their conversation.

"Rich."

"Oh, well," she said, dismissing the subject. "Nobody's perfect."

Ross laughed and seemed to finally agree with her that they had talked enough for one night. He slipped his hand inside her wrapper and found her breast, and Diana shivered with delicious anticipation.

Sensual hunger and passion quickly took precedence over everything else. Her robe disappeared. His khakis landed on the carpeted floor of the sitting room. Ross covered her face, her neck, her breasts, with his kisses. He pressed his mouth into the smooth, satiny skin of her abdomen and ran his hands along the sleek, slender length of her legs. He raised her hips and gave her the most intimate of kisses, and she came apart in his arms, crying out his name, speaking of her love, before she slipped over the edge.

Once she had come back down to earth again, Diana's hands went to his shoulders, her fingers grasping the muscular flesh as her nails scraped sensuously along its surface. She licked her lips and then ventured forth into new territory: she tasted him, the smooth skin, the soft crinkle of private hair, the thrill of his hard, flexed manhood.

When they next kissed they could taste themselves on each other's mouths and lips and tongues. It was seductive. It was erotic. It was provocative. It was impassioned.

Then Ross was there, urging her legs apart, coaxing her to take him, willing her to give all that she had to him. He joined himself to her with a primitive need that Diana craved, welcomed, needed, loved.

He thrust deep into her, making love to her body, to her heart, to her very soul. There was no longer any way to tell where he ended and she began. Their flesh became one. They moved as one. They felt as one. They loved as one.

And when the final shuddering climax took them, Diana heard his name echoing inside her head: Ross. Ross. Ross.

And she heard her name on his lips. "Diana!"

Epilogue

Maybe weddings weren't such a damn waste of time, after all, thought Ross St. Clair as he waited at the front of the church sanctuary.

Not if it was the right time and the right place and the right woman.

Any minute now the organist would play the opening chords of the traditional *Lohengrin* wedding march and the processional would begin.

He stood there, knowing that he would soon see Diana for the first time in her wedding gown. He caught a glimpse of her at the back of the church, and his heart began to pound.

The music started. The guests rose to their feet and turned to watch. The ushers came first, followed by the bridesmaids, including his own sister, Katherine.

Then the flower girl and the ring bearer, and finally the bride on her father's arm.

Tall, blond, coolly chic and utterly beautiful—that was his Diana. But underneath Ross knew there was a very warm and a very sensuous woman.

He never took his eyes from hers as Diana joined him before the minister. The ceremony commenced as the traditional words were recited: "Dearly beloved, we are assembled here in the presence of God, to join this man and this woman in holy marriage..."

And when the clergyman concluded by telling Ross that he could now kiss his bride, he brought his mouth down on Diana's and whispered one word: "Heaven."

* * * * *

Look for NOT *HER* WEDDING! *in December, 1992, only in Silhouette Desire.*

SILHOUETTE® *Desire*™

COMING NEXT MONTH

FREE GIFT OFFER

To receive your free gift, send us the specified number of proofs-of-purchase from any specially marked Free Gift Offer Harlequin or Silhouette book with the Free Gift Certificate properly completed, plus a check or money order (do not send cash) to cover postage and handling payable to Harlequin/Silhouette Free Gift Promotion Offer. We will send you the specified gift.

FREE GIFT CERTIFICATE

ITEM	A. GOLD TONE EARRINGS	B. GOLD TONE BRACELET	C. GOLD TONE NECKLACE
# of proofs-of-purchase required	3	6	9
Postage and Handling	$1.75	$2.25	$2.75
Check one	☐	☐	☐

Name: _____

Address: _____

City: _____ State: _____ Zip Code: _____

Mail this certificate, specified number of proofs-of-purchase and a check or money order for postage and handling to: HARLEQUIN/SILHOUETTE FREE GIFT OFFER 1992, P.O. Box 9057, Buffalo, NY 14269-9057. Requests must be received by July 31, 1992.

PLUS—Every time you submit a completed certificate with the correct number of proofs-of-purchase, you are automatically entered in our MILLION DOLLAR SWEEPSTAKES! No purchase or obligation necessary to enter. See below for alternate means of entry and how to obtain complete sweepstakes rules.

MILLION DOLLAR SWEEPSTAKES
NO PURCHASE OR OBLIGATION NECESSARY TO ENTER

To enter, hand-print (mechanical reproductions are not acceptable) your name and address on a 3" × 5" card and mail to Million Dollar Sweepstakes 6097, c/o either P.O. Box 9056, Buffalo, NY 14269-9056 or P.O. Box 621, Fort Erie, Ontario L2A 5X3. Limit: one entry per envelope. Entries must be sent via 1st-class mail. For eligibility, entries must be received no later than March 31, 1994. No liability is assumed for printing errors, lost, late or misdirected entries.

Sweepstakes is open to persons 18 years of age or older. All applicable laws and regulations apply. Sweepstakes offer void wherever prohibited by law. Prizewinners will be determined no later than May 1994. Chances of winning are determined by the number of entries distributed and received. For a copy of the Official Rules governing this sweepstakes offer, send a self-addressed, stamped envelope (WA residents need not affix return postage) to: Million Dollar Sweepstakes Rules, P.O. Box 4733, Blair, NE 68009.

✂ SD3U

ONE PROOF-OF-PURCHASE
To collect your fabulous FREE GIFT you must include the necessary FREE GIFT proofs-of-purchase with a properly completed offer certificate.

(See inside back cover for offer details)